BEACH SECRETS

BEACH HOUSE ROMANCE, BOOK 3

JULIE CAROBINI

DOLPHIN GATE BOOKS

Beach Secrets
Beach House Romance, Book 3

A previous version of this book was titled *Luke's Second Chance Family*.

Cover design by Kylie Sek

JULIE CAROBINI writes sweet beach romances from her home on the California coast. Please visit her at JulieCarobini.com.

ONCE UPON A TIME …

I wrote a series about five siblings who inherited a beach house—with a catch!

That was in 2020 … and we all know what happened *that* year. Life was turbulent so I decided to do something different: I released all five books under a pen name.

But … I found it difficult to maintain two personas. I also wanted to add a bit more content to these stories. So I pulled the novels from publication, added new scenes, and re-covered the series under my own name.

If you like tropes, such as fake relationships, billionaires, secret babies, and cowboys, then I know you'll love the revised and refreshed Beach House Romance series!

Now, turn the page for book three …

Julie

1

uke froze. The woman he had been avoiding for days—for years, really—was about to cross his path. He continued to trudge along the sidewalk toward his surf shop, drinking the coffee he'd just picked up from the new bakery in town, his baseball cap pulled snugly down on his head. When he reached her, he would look into her eyes, say hello, and get the whole thing over with as fast as possible.

Maggie hadn't changed much at all—still beautiful, curvy, and walked like she owned—or could buy—the entire block. He noted, with startling recall, that she still held her purse the way she had as a teen: arm bent at the elbow in a forty-five degree angle, the handbag dangling from her forearm, a slight shimmy in her gait. Heat crept into his face. How had something like that stuck in his head all this time?

He braced for impact, but the woman's gaze was somewhere else. "Eva?" she was saying, her eyes focused on a young girl in front of her with long, dark hair. "Wait for me, hon."

The girl, slightly taller than his own daughter, skipped on ahead. Luke had heard that Maggie had a daughter, and for a moment, his brain wandered to what might have been. And yet, he had no regret. Well, technically, he regretted his behavior from long ago, but that was something he could never take back. In the end, he did not regret how it all turned out. He couldn't.

His pastor had been helping him find his way through his past.

The little girl went inside the bakery that he had just left, the one that sat like a cream puff in the middle of the block. The new place in Colibri Beach had filled a need in this tired old town, providing a spot to gather that wasn't strewn with old wallpaper and folding chairs. He still wasn't sure about all that pink on the walls, though ...

As the woman passed him by, he glanced up, the coffee cup to his lips, his gaze over the top of it. She didn't notice him, though, which caused him to feel something unexpected. What he expected he would feel was relief, the kind of relief a person encountered when they had been holding their breath underwater for too long and finally surfaced and let it out.

Instead, the sense that rose in his gut reminded him of something wholly different, and as he considered it, he realized what it was. When Maggie Holloway failed to notice him standing feet away from her, Luke felt deep and utter ... disappointment.

He twisted his lips. Served him right. Luke may have been avoiding Maggie for the past decade or so, but when she passed him by with zero recognition on her face, he realized he had received a comeuppance of sorts, the long-time-coming kind. He shook his head slowly. At least she hadn't sneered at him, though he couldn't deny that he probably deserved that too.

Luke watched the doorway of that bakery for a moment after the girl, followed by Maggie, slipped inside, blissfully unaware of his scrutiny. He sighed, threw back the rest of his coffee, then crushed his cup and tossed it into the garbage can on the sidewalk. Quickly, he hopped off the curb and crossed the street, unlocking the storefront he'd acquired nearly five years before.

In a relatively short time, he had made great strides with his surfboard shop. Inside, his footfalls echoed through the space. He flipped a few switches until the place came to life, the smell of wax and sand and saltwater burning his nostrils. His eyes scanned the walls of the shop. In the front, finished boards in varying sizes hung on racks, waiting for buyers to snap them up. But it was the back of the shop that called to him, ever since that summer that Maggie had challenged him to face his fear and dive into the wide and chilly ocean.

What happened in the ensuing years was less easy to recall. The early morning rides, the contests, the girls—lots and lots of girls. And the fear he kept in check—until he no longer could. He shut his eyes, remembering.

"You all right?"

Luke spun around. When had Zack come in? He released a breath and waved the teen inside. "Sorry, dude. Was thinking."

Zack laughed. "My dad does that all the time."

He faltered. "Thinks?"

The kid cracked up. "Stares into space like he can't find his glasses or something."

Luke's smile fell. "Ah." He cleared his throat, not sure how his thirty-year-old self felt to be compared to someone's much-older dad. "So. What can I help you with today?"

Zack handed him a flyer. "I gotta job handing out these flyers for the Ringer Surf Classic. I get extra if I can get stores to tape a flyer to the window. You in?"

Luke ran his eyes over the announcement about the first-time, amateur competition in their small beach town. He grimaced. Not too many decent hotels around here, so he guessed the vacation rentals would be going for a premium. This kind of thing was great for business, but not without its problems. His eyes caught on the list of prizes.

He looked up. "Two-thousand-dollar prize in each category? And all the rest of the prize money to charity? Really?"

Zack whistled. "Yup. Even old timers like you can win a bunch of cash."

"No, thanks."

"What are you ... chicken?" Zack cackled like an old man, rather than a fifteen-year-old with a smart mouth.

Luke focused a mock glare on the kid. "Want my help or not?"

"Sorry."

Luke loved the sport—the smells, the tricks, those serendipitous rides that took a person by surprise. Only he loved them from the sidelines now. Though he owned this shop and had become one of the best board shapers in the area, Luke had not surfed in years. Nor did he intend to start.

"Hey, you could enter and win money for your shop." He looked around. "This place needs some stuff."

"Yeah? Like what kind of stuff?"

"Candy machines, free ice cream, a skate ramp out back ..."

Luke gave Zack another bogus frown. "Not happening."

He'd bought the building that housed his shop long before he knew much about handling finances. Shoot, he'd practically been a kid when he bought it. One thing was for sure: Luke hadn't planned on the high number of repairs he would have to make, the cost of which had shocked him with each invoice. Still, he'd managed quite well.

Luke took a second glance at the flyer in his hands. That prize money would sure come in handy for somebody, though. He perused the list of charities on the flyer. In addition to the usual ocean-centered ones, a charity that helped foster kids had made the cut.

"Then again," he said, "this is pretty rad."

"Epic. So you'll put it on your window?"

Luke screwed up his mouth. "Yeah. Get outta here."

Zack called out "Awesome!" and tore out of the shop, hopped into the street, and zig-zagged his way toward the bakery. Luke shook his head, slight laughter coming from him. The kid was probably off to find himself more sugar since he so obviously lacked energy today.

Luke grabbed a roll of clear tape from a drawer, found an empty spot on the shop's window, and put the competition flyer at teen eye-level. No doubt the surf kids around here would be gawking at that flyer in no time, stirring up all kinds of excitement in Colibri. He stood back and idly rubbed the scar above his lip, grateful for the much-needed distraction.

As he did, Luke caught sight of the bakery across the street ... the one currently holding a piece of his past.

A muffin top never sounded so good.

MAGGIE RUBBED DRIED paint from her chin with the back of her thumb, silently wondering how safe it was to be out in public on such a sunny day. Since moving back to Colibri Beach temporarily, she'd kept herself—and her daughter, Eva—relatively busy and tucked away from the towns' flapping mouths and gaping eyes.

All she wanted to do was make it through the month unscathed by rumor. Oh, and to find a new apartment and work to go home to in Arizona when this was all over.

Thing was, she was struggling. Maggie liked order. Compartmentalizing her life. Not this daily chaos of being scattered on the sea breeze. Already, she felt as if she might crack.

Eva skipped ahead and disappeared into Brooke's Beachside Bakery—the place that Maggie had heard about unceasingly from her sister, Grace, and brother, Jake, both of whom had already spent their required month at the family beach house. She'd been budgeting since she arrived back in Colibri, and though the thought of spending money at the friendly neighborhood bakery wasn't top on her list, her daughter brightened about the prospect. So she soldiered on.

Maggie entered the shop, the aroma of dough and sugar and other pleasing spices enveloping her senses. She licked her lips, enticed by all the chocolatey, sugary goodness staring back at her. If she were at home, far from here, she'd watch herself. First, for money reasons, but mostly, because she wanted to keep her love handles to a minimum.

Eva pointed at the chalkboard sign with words written in a flourish:

"If you love someone, let them go. If they come back with coffee, it was meant to be." - Anonymous

EVA TWISTED a look up at her. "What does that mean, momma?"

A woman behind the counter wearing a name tag that read *Lea* cut in. "It's our ode to coffee, so to speak. And to love," she said with a wink.

Eva scrunched her nose. "I don't like coffee. Do you have hot chocolate?"

Lea laughed. "Sure do." She looked at Maggie. "And for you?"

"I'll have the coffee," Maggie said. She didn't add anything about love because, frankly, her luck in that area was pitiful. Thankfully, though she'd loved and lost more than once, she had gained her beautiful and spunky daughter in the midst of it all. An amazing tradeoff that made her grateful despite the desperate positions she often seemed to find herself in.

She glanced again at the case overflowing with goodies. "And I think I'll also have a chocolate chip muffin top, too."

Eva rose up on her tiptoes. "Can I have an eclair? Please?"

Maggie ran a hand down her daughter's soft brunette locks. Eva had been torn from her home and friends practically overnight, but she had been a trouper. Maggie marveled at the way her ten-year-old had matured during the drama. "Sure. You worked hard, so yes. Pick the one you want."

Eva pointed at the fattest chocolate eclair in the case. "I'll take that one." She then turned her doe eyes up toward her momma. "You worked hard, too. You should get two muffin tops."

Maggie laughed. "Maybe if I had your metabolism, I would."

Eva frowned. "Metabo ... what?"

"Never mind. Why don't you go pick a table while I pay for our snack."

Lea eyed the girl as she bounded across the shop. "Your daughter is so sweet. You seem familiar to me. Have we met?"

"Probably when we were kids. I'm Maggie Holloway and—"

"Oh! One of the Holloway kids. So good to see you again. I'm Lea—I'm close to Jake's age, so you probably don't remember me."

Lea had called her "kid"—how funny was that? Unfortunately, the woman with the animated expression was right—Maggie didn't remember her at all. She didn't want to be rude. Truth was, she had largely forgotten a lot about all those summers spent at Colibri Beach. Or maybe she had just put those days out of her mind. Far, far out of her mind.

"Forgive me," Maggie said. "But there's been a lot of life lived since I spent my summers in Colibri." She didn't care to mention that this beach town was home to what some might refer to as her biggest mistake ever. "I take it you grew up here?"

"Yes, ma'am. Born and raised. My friend Brooke owns this place. I just help her out part-time."

Maggie glanced around the bakery, taking in the burst of pink hues on the walls. The aromas mixed with light, bright colors made her want to prolong her stay, but duty called. She slid a gaze back to Lea. "I can see why you'd want to work here. My parents would have loved this place."

Lea's smile dimmed. "I was so sorry to hear about their accident. My condolences."

"Thank you very much." Her parents' deaths in a car accident had shocked Maggie and her siblings. When they were still reeling from the news, which included revelations about their mother's deteriorating mental condition, another shock had been handed to them: their parents had left everything to charity.

Everything except the family beach house.

Initially, she and her siblings thought they would sell the whole place and split the revenue—something Maggie welcomed given her perilous financial state. But their parents had other plans for them. And if they didn't follow through with their parents' wishes? The house would also be given to charity.

No exceptions.

Lea tilted her head. "How is the house coming along?"

Maggie raised her brows, momentarily silenced. Apparently, word had gotten around this small community. The idea that people were talking about them—about *her*—made something in her gut crimp.

Lea continued, a tinge of red on her cheeks now. "I mean, I-I heard that you're all fixing it up to sell. Isn't that right?"

"It is. We'll sell eventually. I guess you heard about our parents' crazy will."

Lea bit her bottom lip. "That each of you has to stay in the house for a month? And that you all have to do your part to fix it up?"

Maggie exhaled, nodding. There really were few secrets in this town ...

"Yes," Lea continued, her head bobbing. "I heard."

"I see. Well, we still have a ways to go. Grace cleaned the place very well and gave us our marching orders. Jake started with the kitchen—it's gorgeous, by the way. And my job is to paint as much as possible." Maggie held up a paint-spattered hand. "I am working on the main floor bath, which Jake also updated."

Lea both cringed and laughed. "Then you deserve a double shot of coffee. Listen, why don't you join your daughter at the table and I'll bring everything over to you."

"Thanks. That would be perfect." Maggie made her way to the table in the corner where Eva sat patiently waiting.

"I think I'm going to like it around here," Eva said, a smile on her impish face.

Maggie laughed. "Oh really."

"We don't have any beaches near our house in Arizona. Only donut shops. Yeah, I like it here."

"I'm glad." Maggie took a surreptitious look around. "I like it too."

Lea showed up carrying a platter with multiple muffin

tops, two eclairs, a tall mug of steaming coffee, and a mug of hot chocolate with too many marshmallows to count.

Eva squealed when the eclairs were set in front of her while Maggie gasped.

Lea smiled. "I doubled your order—consider it a welcome to town gift. Anything else I can get you?"

Maggie looked up. "Point me toward a gym? I think I'm going to need one."

Lea cracked up. "Not necessary—if only I looked as good as you. Your hair is gorgeous, too."

"My mom's a hairdresser," Eva said, chocolate smeared across her cheek.

Lea's eyes widened. "Really?" She touched her ponytail in a self-conscious way. "Maybe you could help me with this mop sometime. It's really pretty unmanageable."

"I'd be happy to, though I would not call your pretty hair a mop."

Lea slid into a chair next to her and leaned onto the table. "Really? Because I never know what to do with it, you know? So I always end up just pulling it into this dumb ponytail."

Eva giggled. "Dumb ponytail ..."

Unable to help herself, Maggie inspected Lea's hair. She'd been fiddling with hair since she was a kid, so her profession had been a natural choice. That and the flexibility it offered to a single mother.

The bell on the bakery's front door rang, signaling a customer had entered. Lea sighed and dragged herself out of the chair. "I've got to get that, but maybe I could stop by the house sometime and talk to you?"

Maggie nodded. "Of course. Any time."

After Lea had left, Maggie wrapped her hands around her mug of coffee, willing herself to keep her mind away from worries. She didn't dare think about all the clients she would have to try and reconnect with when she moved back home. Her salon had closed abruptly more than a month ago and she had been unable to secure a new space ever since.

She nibbled on one of the muffin tops, her spinning mind unable to slow down and enjoy the respite. When she had first learned about the strange requirements in their parents' will, Maggie had been so frustrated. How in the world would she find the time to take a month off of work and travel to California to babysit the house that they had vacationed in every summer of her young life? Sure it sounded like a fun idea, but ideas and reality were two different things.

Then the salon's shutdown happened, followed by an eviction notice from her apartment landlord since she had, unfortunately, been unable to keep up with the rent. She bit back a sigh. As it turned out, the timing for her stay at the beach house was pretty perfect, well, except for the memories she still chose to forget.

Maggie took a sip of coffee, grateful for the time to consider her options before jumping back into the fray of life. As she peeked over her coffee cup at the sweet daughter she'd been blessed to call her own, she wondered what they would do when their month at the beach house was up.

LUKE KEPT HIS HEAD DOWN, making his order list for nearly a half hour, when a commotion caused his chin to jerk up. He squinted toward the front window of his shop. The young girl he had seen enter the bakery earlier flew out much like Zack had when he ran out of the shop this morning.

To his chagrin, Maggie followed closely behind her. She shaded her eyes and scanned the block, her gaze brushing over the shop's open door.

Luke took a step back from the counter and bit back a scowl. He had a business to run and no time to run to or from the past. Maybe he should have stayed in the back today and focused on the *blank*—that piece of foam that had been staring him in the eyes for days—waiting for him and challenging him to shape it.

He craned his neck, stretching to see if they had disappeared. Instead, the little girl punched a fist into her waist and swiveled a look back at Maggie. She righted herself then and made a beeline for his shop, casting a quick look in either direction before crossing the street.

It was too late to turn the Open sign to Closed, right? Too late to slam the door shut?

What are you ... chicken?

Though he wanted to run, Luke stood his ground as Maggie and her daughter approached. Instead of coming inside, though, the girl planted herself in front of the newly posted sign on his window, her eyes widening.

She swiveled toward Maggie. "Surf contest. Can we watch it?"

Maggie frowned. "We'll be gone by then, punkin. Sorry."

"Aw!"

Luke dropped his gaze to the papers on his counter. He

perused his order list for the tenth time: wax, shop T-shirts, stickers, and flip-flops in size twelve. He rubbed that spot on his upper lip, feeling like a fool. He'd loved Maggie once, but it was a long time ago, and frankly? As a stupid kid he hadn't known what love was, so even if they had somehow stayed together, he probably would have messed it up.

And he wouldn't have his daughter Siena now.

He kept his head down, though his ears were perked.

"Can we go inside?" Eva said.

Maggie hesitated for a beat before relenting.

Luke met them head on. "Hello."

She let go of her handbag but swiftly caught it before it hit the floor. Eva, however, didn't seem to notice, the girls' gaze pointed unwavering on the stack of boogie boards Luke kept in a corner of the store.

"Mom," she said, "can I get one of these?"

Maggie's mouth gaped and she slid a glance toward her daughter.

Eva continued, "The one in the garage is super gross and crackly all over. It has dirt and webs on it, too."

Luke noticed the way Maggie's forehead wrinkled, caught between acknowledging him and answering her daughter. He broke the silence and stepped toward the stack of boards.

"Here," he said, plucking a red and white one from the bunch. "This one's a good size for you. Want to take a look?"

Eva nodded.

He watched as she took the board from him and ran her hand across its surface. "Have you boogie boarded before?"

She shook her head no, vehemently.

He smiled. "Well, then, you're about to have some fun."

Maggie interrupted them. "Hello, Luke."

He pulled his attention away from Eva and gave her a slight nod. "Maggie."

Eva frowned and looked at her mom. "How come you know his name?"

"We were friends when I was ... your age."

He was having a difficult time taking his eyes off of Maggie, but he forced himself to snap a look at Eva, the girl a mini version of her mother. "Bet you think that was a long time ago," he said, putting his hand out. "I'm Luke, by the way."

Eva giggled and shook it. "It's kinda weird to think of my mom as a kid. I bet she was bossy."

Maggie stabbed her waist with her hand, much like Eva had done earlier. "That's enough, Eva."

Eva bit her lip, but he could tell by the light in the girl's eyes that she knew she wasn't in serious trouble. As for what Maggie thought of him after all these years, he couldn't tell.

Luke chuckled. "I wouldn't call her bossy, Eva. She always liked to speak her mind, though."

Eva looked serious. "Yeah. She has a lot to say."

"Oh brother." Maggie shook her head. "I was just trying to keep order around this town. Somebody had to protect the beach from all the year-rounders."

Luke scratched his chin. "Year-rounders? That a word?"

"If weekenders is, then yes. It's a word."

He grinned. "As I recall, you showed up on the first day of summer every year and staked your claim." Luke slid a look at Eva. "Your mom had her favorite beach chair—it was blue. She'd set it up under that tattered old umbrella your parents had, and woe to anyone who would sit in it without permission!"

Maggie shook her head in disapproval, though her eyes danced. "Usually stinky boys who just wanted to mess with my things."

Luke quieted, a smile lingering. "Or get your attention."

Something hardened in her gaze. She dropped that fist from her waist and snapped a look toward Eva. "I don't think we'll have much time for that, kiddo."

"Aw, please? Can't I try it?"

Maggie shook her head. "Maybe another time ... if I get all my work done at the house. Okay?"

"Okay." Reluctantly, Eva handed back the board.

Luke took it with regret. He watched as Eva twirled off to another part of the shop, her attention turned to the rack of short boards he'd created last spring.

"She's a sweet kid," he said.

Maggie hitched her purse onto the crook of her elbow, as if readying to leave. She swung a gaze at her daughter. "She's my everything."

He lowered his voice now, drawn to her in such a big way that it surprised him. "How are you, Maggie?"

She hesitated before dragging her gaze back to him. Her eyes were duller somehow. "I'm ... great. In a good place. I'm at the family home, carrying out my parents' wishes by doing my share—I'm painting several rooms—and giving Eva a taste of my childhood the best way I can."

"I'm sorry about your parents."

She nodded, her expression unreadable, and he wondered how often she had been reminded of them since she'd come home—whether from people like him bringing it up or familiar memories that she had likely encountered. It had to be tough.

He knew it had been for him whenever people asked him about his wife.

"Thank you," she said.

"I saw Grace a couple of months ago," Luke said. "Did she mention it?"

Maggie gave him a vague shrug and stepped back, her gaze drifting to Eva who stood mesmerized by the boards. Her body language was telling and he shut off the spigot of questions that suddenly filled his mind. Like, why did you run off with ... that guy? If I had apologized, would you have come back? And most important, could you ever forgive me for how I treated you?

She took a step back, as if reading his mind, a tension wrinkle between her eyes. Maybe ... just maybe it was best that he not bring up all that old stuff.

His eyes flitted to Eva and he knew the answer: Now was not the right time to talk about old hurts. Maybe there never would be one.

Eva's voice split the silence between Luke and Maggie. "So I'm thinking ... maybe I should take surfing lessons, momma. Did you know there's a surf camp here?"

Maggie's eyes widened, as if stricken. She was no longer a carefree teen, that he could tell. And though he, too, had moved on, it ached to see what had been lost. Growing up had a way of chasing away the happy-go-lucky days.

She walked over to her daughter and gently placed a hand on her back. Together they stood looking up at the boards that Luke had shaped himself. He couldn't take his eyes off her.

Maggie leaned her head down closer to Eva, giving her back a brief rub. "I'm sorry, darlin', I would love for you to surf sometime, but it's not in my budget right now."

Eva nodded. Was she used to this answer? Luke frowned and quirked a look toward the stack of boogie boards he kept on hand for the tourists that invariably flocked in during the summer, looking for things to keep their kids busy and ... carefree.

Instinctively, he grabbed the board he had shown Eva earlier. "How about you take this and see how you do with it? My treat."

Maggie's face clouded over and she shook her head, but Eva moved quickly across the space. She reached for the board, her face lighting up. "Really?"

"Yup." He pressed his lips into a smile, working to keep his gaze connected with Maggie's. "A gift for a ... bossy old friend."

Eva giggled.

Maggie did not look too pleased at all and her tone turned testy. "I'm sure your boss wouldn't appreciate you giving away the store. What are you doing here, anyway, Luke? Don't you have some waves to watch?"

"I own this place." Luke dipped his chin, his eyes connecting with hers. "You know I was teasing you earlier. Not about the board—that's a gift. But about the bossy thing."

Maggie shook her head. "I just—"

"Please, momma." Eva batted big brown eyes at her mother and held the boogie board to her chest.

Luke almost felt guilty. Almost.

Maggie set her chin, a slight glare cast Luke's way. She

licked her lips and returned her gaze to Eva. "Hon, it's just one more thing we'll have to move. Besides, we played hooky this morning, but there might not be too much more free time over the next few weeks. I'd hate for you to be sad every time you look at the thing."

Eva jumped slightly, her excitement palpable. "I won't! I promise!" She turned to him, still hugging that board to her body. "Thank you, Luke!"

That guilt Luke was feeling set in fast now. But shoot. It was just a boogie board. Every kid needed one, didn't they? Reflexively, he pulled off his baseball cap and ran a hand through his bedhead.

Maggie gasped.

He laughed, sheepishly. "Guess I should've run a brush through it before opening the shop."

"Wait ... are you dying your hair now, Luke?" She seemingly lost all thought of the boogie board and stepped closer to him, her eyes squinting and peering at his head.

"She does that all the time," Eva said, a slight roll of her eyes.

"Hush, you," Maggie said. She returned her gaze to his head. "It looks so natural. Who does it?"

"What in the world? Nobody." He slapped the hat back onto his head and pulled the bill down low while tugging it tighter in the back. "Why are you so interested in my head?"

Eva spoke up, laughter in her voice. "Mom's a hairdresser. She's interested in everybody's head."

Luke tipped his chin up and let out a laugh, too. "Oh. Okay. Makes sense. I guess." He pulled the hat back off his head and tossed it on the counter. "This is the real me. Didn't even wash it today."

"Gross," Eva said.

He turned and stuck his tongue out at her, enjoying the banter. If she were one of the locals, she'd probably be in here weekly during the summers and on weekends the rest of the year. Lots of kids called this place home-away-from-home. He wouldn't have it any other way. No matter how surfing ended for him, the sport helped him keep his nose clean when he might have otherwise found himself in all kinds of trouble.

Maggie's stricken expression hadn't changed, though, and he was beginning to wonder if he looked worse than he thought. When he was a kid, his mother would get after him for not washing his hair, but he'd always thought, *why bother?* Back then, he always rolled out of bed and hit the surf, saturating his hair with salt water and sand anyway.

She stepped slightly closer, her voice hushed. "I thought you were more ... blond."

He pulled back, one hand finding his chest, a grin stuck on his face. "You're kidding."

She stared at him, her brows dipping low over her eyes. "You look so different. I-I change people's hair color all the time, but wow. You really look like ... someone else."

"I'm the same guy, Mags," he said, calling her by the name she once answered to. "I just don't use Sun-Dash anymore."

Maggie flinched a little.

"Used to spray that stuff all over myself and then bake out in the sun all summer long." He leaned closer and winked. "I don't recommend it."

"What's Sun-Dash?" Eva asked.

Maggie stepped closer to her daughter. "It's hair bleach that works with the sun and you should never, ever try it."

Luke cut in. "Was popular in surf culture, though I don't promote it or sell it here."

"Yes," Maggie continued, looking at Eva. "If you want to change your hair, you should—"

"I know, I know. Always go to you." Eva pouted at Luke. "She's still mad at me for cutting my bangs."

Maggie smiled slightly. She pulled her daughter into a one-arm hug and Luke sensed a lightening of the mood.

"Well," Maggie said, "we'd better go. You sure about the board?"

He grinned. "Absolutely. Maybe I'll see you two out on the beach sometime, eh, Mags? You need a break once in a while from all that painting, don't you think?"

Maggie shrugged, her eyes not meeting his. "Maybe. Thanks, Luke."

"Nice seeing you again," he said.

She nodded but didn't say anything more. Given their history, what else could he expect?

2

M aggie walked along unseeing, her mind
preoccupied. She had violated her better judg-
ment and was now paying the price. Maybe on
the way back they should stop at the store and pick up baked
goods so that the next time she and Eva needed a break,
they'd stay home.

Who was she kidding? Running into Luke was bound to
happen. From what she knew, which wasn't much, Luke
Hunter still lived here in Colibri. He wasn't on social media
—she'd looked, much to her shame—but occasionally an
old acquaintance would mention him in their banal post.

Still, Maggie had hoped to duck into Colibri, fulfill her
part of the infamous Last Will and Testament, and slide back
out with her heart intact. Those plans were dashed the
minute she looked up and realized that her ex-boyfriend
owned the surf shop that she and Eva had wandered into.

She bit the inside of her cheek. Had she been right to
stay in there and banter with Luke as if they didn't have a

past? Especially with the secret she still harbored? She mentally shook off the weight of guilt that haunted her. Dashing out of there would have seemed suspicious, and rude. And it would not have changed a thing. Luke was a happily married man and she wasn't about to do anything to change that.

She had promised.

"He's a super nice man, isn't he?" Eva asked the question, breaking into her thoughts as they crossed the street. Maggie nodded, then watched her daughter skip ahead, as she usually did. Only this time she was dragging a boogie board along.

Maggie exhaled. Her desire to get out a little and see the town turned into an eventful morning. She passed by the bakery and took a quick peek in the window. The cute place was teeming with people and for a second she almost wanted to go back in for another pour of coffee. Her stop in there already felt miles away.

Maggie shook off her melancholy the best she could, unable to get thoughts of seeing Luke again out of her mind. She didn't want to admit this, even privately, but she had thought of him often during the past decade—a little too often. He hurt her deeply back then, but replaying the events of that night also served to highlight her own poor choices.

Kind of a lose-lose situation.

Maggie blew out another breath, releasing the tension that had built up during their short time in the surf shop. Luke had been nice. And funny. And too generous.

It was annoying.

Good thing he was married.

Though she wanted to hang onto the anger that lingered

within her, a fresh and frightening thought entered her consciousness as she trudged along. She flicked a look at her daughter, desperately wanting to protect their life together. Her mind began to race, but she carefully avoided the rising fear. Instead, she flicked away the crush of thoughts in her mind, not allowing them to flourish.

One thing Maggie *had* been happy about was how easily she had snuffed out Eva's interest in surfing. So much to unpack there. Thankfully, though, it did not appear that she would need to address it. In some weird way, she had Luke to thank for that. At first, the gift of a boogie board made her cringe. She wasn't a charity case. She did not need some ex-boyfriend to assuage his guilt by giving her gifts.

As she thought about it, though, she hoped the gift would satisfy her vivacious daughter for the next four weeks —exactly the time they had left in Colibri. Guilt had already snaked through her. Wasn't this trip out to the bakery—and ultimately, to the surf shop—to appease just that? She felt guilty about her single-parent home. That they were suddenly uprooted. And that Maggie had brought her beautiful daughter to a veritable playground at the beach where she didn't have a friend—and Maggie had little time to entertain her.

Inside the house that her family had called home for many, many summers, Maggie dumped her purse and yoga jacket on the bench at the end of the hall. She still couldn't get used to coming in the front door off the driveway. For some reason, memories of bounding down the hall and exiting the house through the back door that led to a rickety old deck on the sand and her mom's pink bench gave her comfort. Like she was still young and without worry.

"Can I keep the boogie board in my room?" Eva asked her, holding the shiny new toy in front of her.

"For now. After you use it for the first time, you'd better keep it under the deck. Otherwise, you'll be sweeping every day."

"O-kay, Mom."

Maggie reached out as Eva attempted to pass her. She corralled her with one arm, gently, and pulled her back to her. Then she smacked a kiss on her head. "I love you."

"Love you, too. Going to my room now, 'k?"

Maggie watched her go. The room she referred to was the most popular in the house with its mint green walls and oversized white comforter with a big blue whale on it. A smile reached her lips. Man, did she and her sisters fight over that room. Usually two were in it, sometimes just one. All four girls had stayed there at one time or another, but their brother, Jake, never had. He had since worn that fact as a badge of honor. "Too girly," he always said.

She peeked inside. Eva was lying on her stomach, headphones on, bobbing to some beat. The boogie board was on the floor in the corner, several stuffed animals curled up on it. Maggie's smile grew. Her daughter was experiencing the same "affliction" they all had. Every single one of them had found time for idle play in the old house, long beyond the maximum age for that sort of thing. It's what life here brought.

This was probably the same reason she met Luke and chased after him the way she did. The thought caused her to roll her hands into fists and dig her fingernails into her palms. "Ugh!"

Eva peeked out of her bedroom. "Did you say something, Mom?"

Maggie shook her head and continued heading down the hall toward the kitchen. "It was nothing, Eva. Go back to your music."

She had to get ahold of herself. Truth was, her random meetup with Luke brought with it memories she didn't care to relive, realities long buried. Exactly the reason it bothered her so much that he was able to so easily jump back into conversation without mention of why they hadn't spoken a word since ... that fateful night.

She stood with her hip against the kitchen island, newly covered in quartz. Jake had done an amazing job with this room and she was the first one, other than him, to benefit from it. But it didn't change the fact that, at this moment, she was currently unnerved. She wanted nothing more than to blame Luke for the sins of the past, but if she had learned nothing else in the last dozen years, it's that they had been young. Stupid. Full of hope for a future that had been quickly doused by a flood of *life happens*.

Still, she wanted to blame him. A couple of times today, a troubled look seemed to cross Luke's face. In those moments she thought, *hey, maybe he remembers my heartbreak. And he's sorry.*

She closed her hand and studied her fingernails. Luke never actually said those words to her, though. Not that it mattered. Why was she so hyper-focused on this now? After so many years?

Her mouth went dry and she reached for the fridge, pulled out a can of Perrier and drank it down so fast it burned her throat. She tossed the can into the recycle bin and stared into space for a few seconds before pushing herself to get moving. She put her hand on her lower back and stretched lightly.

Several areas of the house needed a fresh coat of paint and she was determined to do her part. But Maggie had more than painting to do—she had to find a job back home. And a place to live. After her brother's revelation about his financial status, she knew she had something to fall back on and that gave her some semblance of peace

But ... relying on somebody else when she was as able-bodied as them? Not her style.

She just likes to speak her mind ...

Luke's words ripped through her because she knew it was true. And yet, she had stood there today like a wooden door, creaking occasionally, but never fully coming alive to say what she meant to say. Or wanted to say.

What was happening to her?

Her cell phone rang, jarring her from that deep dark hole she was spiraling into. Jake's name blared on the screen.

"Hey, sis."

"Hey, yourself." Maggie righted herself, pushing all thoughts of Luke, past and present, away from her mind.

"Making a ten-course meal in my new kitchen yet?"

She quirked a smile. "You mean 'our' new kitchen."

He laughed. "Gotcha. How are things? Really."

"Jake Holloway, I've never known you to be so interested in my life. What's up?"

He coughed his protest. "I beg your pardon. I'm *always* interested in my sisters' lives."

"Uh-huh."

"So ... how's the painting coming? You have enough paint? Brushes? Tarps?"

Maggie exhaled and shut her eyes. He was checking up on her? Really? She bit back a retort and instead said, "Yes to all three."

"So ... you've got some done, then."

"I do."

"And the walls are a nice light shade of Swiss Coffee or similar, right?"

She wagged her head now, truly irritated. Two men in one day had managed to thoroughly annoy her. Imagine that. "Sheesh, Jake! Everyone's always on my case about being controlling and they have it all wrong—you're the one!"

His laughter rumbled. "Okay, I give. I know how much you girls want to sell the place. If only Mom and Dad hadn't drawn up that crazy will. Drives me nuts that I can't just send a crew over there and be done with it."

"Nice problem to have, though, don't you think?"

He was quiet a moment. "It is."

Maggie ran her fingers through her hair and tucked a few strands behind her ear. "Just know everything is under control, Jake. No worries at all." That wasn't completely true, if she counted her "chance" meeting with Luke, the one she couldn't seem to shake from her head.

But she continued, "I'll catch you all up tomorrow on our weekly phone call." The five Holloway kids had been scattered to various cities for some time, but after their parents' untimely death and subsequent will restrictions, they had made it a point to meet for a weekly video call to keep everyone updated.

"Sounds good," he said. "Guess I'll let you go then."

Eva wandered into the kitchen looking bored. Already. She opened the pantry door, plucked two pieces of chocolate from a gift box Jake had left them, and attempted to leave. Maggie held her hand out. Eva rolled her eyes, handed her mother one of the candies, and started to walk off.

Again, Maggie held up a hand to stop her. "Hang on a sec, Jake. Eva wants to say hello to her uncle."

After handing off the phone to Eva, Maggie headed down the hall where dingy walls and a couple of hours of work greeted her.

JAKE WAS RIGHT. Twenty-four hours had passed since her brother called and Maggie found herself swooning in the beach house's new kitchen. She never meant to rely on take-out as much as she had in the past, but her rental kitchen was the pits, frankly. She hated eating in it, let alone putting raw food on any of its surfaces.

She inhaled and took in the quartz, the sea-inspired handles, the shiny new appliances. Maggie blinked, thankful, and still shocked, that her brother had been able to wrangle his vendors for good prices for all of this.

One thing she wasn't surprised about was that he could install everything. Jake and their father had fought for years, with Jake leaving the family business to study architecture. She never really understood why the two sole men in her family couldn't get along. To her it always seemed they were speaking the same language.

Maybe that was the problem. So busy talking that neither one heard the other.

"We having mac and cheese tonight?" Eva asked.

She planned to make a quick dinner and clean up before the weekly call with her siblings, but she was pushing it on the time. "Homemade, yes. Want to help?"

Eva nodded.

"You can measure out the breadcrumbs and the parmesan and mix it all together. I'll let you know when it's time to put it on top of the macaroni."

For the next few minutes they worked side by side, the sound of an occasional wave overpowering the music playing on Maggie's cell phone. After dinner was in the oven to brown, she noticed a voicemail on her phone. The beach area had notoriously spotty cell service, so the call probably never even rang.

Maggie frowned. The message was from Luke's surf shop.

"Knock, knock!" Daisy Mcafee peeked her head through the open front door. "Hi, girls!"

Eva perked up and jogged over to the door. "Aunt Daisy!"

Daisy hugged her soon-to-be niece. The "girl next door" had recently become engaged to Jake, gaining mad respect from all four of his sisters. They'd all wondered who would be the one to tame that man's heart.

"You want to have mac and cheese with us?" Eva asked.

Maggie nodded. The video call with her siblings would be happening soon and it would be fun for Daisy to be on the call with her. "Please. There's tons of it and I'm already regretting all the cheese I'm going to eat."

"Sure! You mind if I bring a friend?"

Maggie's brows rose. Daisy's mother, Wren, lived next door and she'd recently experienced a stroke, which is what brought Daisy back to Colibri in the first place. "Is your mother feeling well enough to join us?"

"Oh, no. That's not what I meant. Sorry. She's already in bed for the night. I meant—"

Jake burst through the door. "She meant me!"

Eva catapulted into his arms. "Uncle Jake!"

Maggie tilted her head. "What the ..."

Daisy opened her palms with a little shrug. "What can I say? He missed me."

"Or maybe you stopped by to spy on my paint job," Maggie said.

Jake's mouth popped open. "So paranoid."

Maggie clucked her tongue. "Whatever. Mac and cheese is in the oven." She turned toward the kitchen. "I'm about to make a salad, so feel free to spy all you like."

He gave Eva another squeeze before setting her back on the floor. Annoyed as she was at Jake's nosiness, she had to admit how grateful she was that Eva had a good man in her life to look up to. She practically worshipped her uncle. "Thought I'd jump on the call with you since I'm here."

"Good idea," Maggie said. The Holloway siblings had fallen into a rhythm with the calls, using them to keep each other up-to-date with the house's progress, and frankly, with their lives. It was the most they had seen each other in years.

Jake snapped his fingers. "By the way, I paid for the surf camp, so you're good to go."

Maggie stopped. She turned around, slowly. "You ... what?"

Jake slid a questioning look at Eva. "You did ask your mother about the surf lessons, right?"

"I did! Remember, Mom? You said we couldn't afford it. You looked so sad, so I asked Uncle Jake on the phone last night and he said he could buy them for me. I wanted to surprise you."

Maggie narrowed her eyes, first at Eva, and then, Jake. "Did you ... did you call Luke Hunter?"

Jake's face still had that confused look on it. "Yes. I called and paid for them over the phone. What's wrong?"

Wordlessly, Maggie spun around and headed toward the fridge. She popped open the door and began pulling out lettuce, carrots, and an avocado, slamming them onto that new counter one by one.

Jake walked up to her, his eyes searching. "Did I screw up?"

"You should've asked me first." She tried to control the shake in her voice, not to mention the threatening tears. In her peripheral vision, she noticed Daisy gently stop Eva, who was trying to escape, and turn her back toward the conversation.

Jake pressed his lips together and nodded.

Maggie turned to Eva. "And you should've asked me too, Eva."

"But I did, Momma."

Maggie shook her head. "I told you that I won't have much time to sit on the beach this visit." *And that lessons weren't in my budget ...*

Eva wrapped her arms around Maggie's waist and turned up her chin. Her big eyes glistened and Maggie had to look away.

Under normal circumstances, Maggie would have been thrilled to send Eva to surf camp. She was young, but every one of her siblings was too when they learned to surf at camp—except Lacy who found a cute surfer to teach her. None of them kept at it, but it was something they could all look back on fondly.

She stroked her daughter's hair, longing to show her there was more to life than work, stress, and drama. Maggie sighed. Surf camp fit that desire to a T. The only issue was ... Luke.

Her breath caught just thinking about him being in Eva's life. Shame heated her skin. She'd been right not to tell him that ... that he had another daughter. She'd made a promise, and breaking that would have hurt so many.

Maggie breathed in deeply. She pulled her daughter in tighter and snapped a look at Jake.

He raised his eyebrows. "We good?"

She rolled her eyes. "No more favors, especially without asking me. *Capiche*?"

Eva lifted her gaze. "What's that mean?"

Jake came over and kissed Eva's head. "It's Italian for 'I'm warning you, little brother.'"

Maggie shook her head. "That's not an exact translation, Eva."

Jake's laughter rumbled through the room. "But it's mighty close!"

Daisy gave him a shove with her hip, laughing. "I hate to break up this little debate, you two, but Maggie, I was wondering if you'd be willing to do me a favor."

"For you, anything." Maggie stuck her tongue out at Jake, like old times. He snickered.

"Would you be willing to cut my mother's hair? She's doing a lot better after the stroke, but isn't quite comfortable yet with the idea of sitting in a hair salon, you know?"

Maggie nodded as Eva bounded over to the fridge and took out two bottles of salad dressing. "Completely understandable. And, sure, I'll run over there tomorrow. Would that work?"

Daisy hugged her. "You're a lifesaver. Yes! Whatever time works for you. I'm going to set up a new TV for her tomorrow and teach her how to use it. So just let me know when you're coming over and I'll make sure she's ready."

"Will do. Probably late morning—"

Jake winced.

Maggie squinted. "What?"

"That's when you're supposed to take Eva to surf camp."

And, once again, run into Luke ... Maggie turned toward the kitchen so no one would notice her agitation. She grabbed the lettuce from the counter and began to wash it in the sink.

Daisy cut in. "If you can't make it over to my mom's after all—"

"That's not it," Maggie said. "Was just thinking of when would be a better time." She shook the lettuce in the sink, laid it on paper towels, and swiveled a look up at her brother. "Where is it held and what time does Luke want Eva over there?"

"It's walking distance from here, at Segura Beach."

Eva asked, "Oh, it's not at our beach?"

Jake smiled. "The swells are softer up at Segura. There's a sand break there so it's a safer place to learn. Oh, and Eva needs to be there at ten o'clock. By the way, it's not Luke doing the teaching."

"Oh no?" She returned to the island with the lettuce and began to slice carrots as nonchalantly as possible.

"Yeah, he said he's retired from surfing, and when I laughed about that, he told me he was dead serious."

Relief flooded her. Still, what Jake said was strange. Luke not surfing? Fat chance of that.

Then again, he had been the big kahuna around Colibri after winning all those surf contests. Maybe he thought teaching the sport was beneath him now. "I guess he meant that he was done with teaching. That makes more sense."

Jake rubbed the back of his neck, his mouth a flat line. "I don't know. He said surfing. Period."

Maggie rolled her eyes and began tearing up the lettuce and tossing it and the carrots into a bowl. She grabbed a ripe tomato and began dicing it. "Okay, fine. Daisy, how about I stop by your mama's house after Eva's camp—I want to watch the first day."

Eva cut in. "Aw, Mom!"

Maggie stopped the knife working over that tomato, her brows raised. "Take it or leave it."

"Fine."

Daisy gave Maggie a side hug and grabbed a carrot from the cutting board. "I'm so thankful for you, Maggie."

Forty-five minutes later, after their bellies were full, Daisy and Eva cleared the table while Maggie and Jake moved into the living room for the call with their siblings.

Her sister Grace, a lawyer, appeared first on the screen looking fiercely busy, her eyes somewhere else. But her mama-to-be skin glowed.

"Hey, Grace," Maggie said.

Grace's chin jerked up, her eyes peering through glasses

that Maggie hadn't seen before. "Sorry. Working on a brief that's due tomorrow."

Maggie tilted her head. "How's the baby nursery coming along?"

Grace crinkled her forehead momentarily. Her eyes widened and a smile made it to her face. "I've ordered everything online and we'll be getting it set up this weekend. We're going with a cruise ship motif."

Jake spat a laugh. "Tell me you're kidding."

Grace's expression was non-committal. "You'll have to come see it for yourself."

"Well," Maggie cut in, "I'm just glad you're thinking about something other than the law. A baby's gonna turn your world upside down, if you don't already know it."

Grace closed her eyes and sat back. "I do and I'm excited … just so, so busy these days with the firm."

"Hey, y'all," Bella's soft voice cut into the call. She looked rested and dreamy, as always, and Maggie had to wonder if their youngest sister did much other than read books all day while breathing in essential oils floating up from her bedside diffuser.

"How are things, Bella?" Maggie asked.

Bella sighed, dreamily. "It's been a beautiful day. I'm just up from a nap."

Grace spat a sigh and Jake wagged his head, a goofy grin on his face.

A voice cut into the banter. "What're all you losers smirking about?" Lacy, their middle sister, joined the call, irascible as ever.

Maggie quirked a look at her. "Are we keeping you from something?"

Lacy sipped her wine. "This boring ritual is taking me away from my nightly quiet time, yes. Let's get this started, shall we?"

Maggie sighed and looked from sibling to sibling. In some ways, Lacy was right. Their weekly call had become a ritual and a little redundant. Maggie didn't believe in living with regret, but a thought did nag at her: If she and her sisters and brother had come to the house as a group regularly before their parents had died, would all these calls even be necessary?

"Maggie?" Jake caught her attention with one raised eyebrow.

Startled back into the present, she nodded. "You're right, Lacy. Let's get started."

MAGGIE SAT on the tiny back porch of the old beach house, marveling at the swaths of translucent white painted across the sky's light blue canvas. Had the sky always been this gorgeous? Life could have been so different if she had slowed down and thought about the future before making such a life-changing decision about it. What if she had come back here years ago with baby in tow?

She already knew the answer to that. Colibri was too small for that scenario to be anything but messy. Although her marriage ended up disastrous, Maggie would not have wanted Eva to grow up as the talk of the beach.

Perhaps this was partly why her mother had urged her to marry Greg. She'd had the best intentions, despite the eventual outcome ...

Maggie drew swirls on the arm of the faded pink bench, smooth and splinter-free from years of sun and salt. She had to be honest with herself. Maggie had wanted to make her own way—she had always had an independent streak, and though it had yet to pay off, she would not be giving up anytime soon. Regret caught her in the windpipe and she swallowed it down hard. No time for that. Someday, she would be able to support Eva in a nice house like this.

In the meantime, she would tell her daughter tales of growing up here—the good memories of her siblings and parents—and provide her with all the adventure she could scrape up. Even if it killed her.

"Mom?" Eva peered out the back screen door. "Do you think I need my water shoes?"

Maggie smiled despite herself. Eva woke up excited and had been getting ready for an hour, doing what, Maggie wasn't sure. "Just bring a pair of flip-flops in case the sand gets hot," she said. "You probably won't wear them long."

"And you're sure they're going to let me borrow a surfboard?"

"Yes. Uncle Jake confirmed that for me. We good?"

"Good!"

The door slammed shut and Maggie blew out another sigh. Last night, her sisters gave her so much *garbage* for her reticence about letting Eva attend surf camp. Neither Grace nor Bella seemed to realize Maggie's aversion to seeing Luke again, although Lacy gave her more than one knowing glance. At one point, she wanted to reach through the screen and smack that cocky smile off her sister's face.

Instead, Maggie had ignored the often-sardonic looks her sister had cast her way.

In the end, Lacy suggested that Maggie take a "chill pill," and then the rest of the room had a laugh at her expense.

Whatever. Someday they would all be parents, and they would find out then how some decisions were very difficult to make.

The screen door shut again. With a bag hitched over her shoulder, Eva stood waiting, a fat grin on her face. Maggie grabbed a beach bag that she had stocked with snacks, and together they trekked northward along the sand, until Eva ran on ahead.

After several minutes of trudging through thick sand, Maggie's calves began to burn, yet another reminder that she wasn't a freewheeling teen any longer. Sheesh. If she kept up this line of thinking, her almost-thirty self would start acting like the new ... fifty.

She picked up the pace, determined not to let something as small as pulled calf muscles ruin her day. Plenty of other scenarios could manage that. Maggie still had a hard time believing that she had allowed her daughter and her brother to convince her to add this detour into her schedule ... her sisters' admonishments not forgotten.

At least Luke wouldn't be teaching her kid. Though she'd never told her daughter about how she had once felt about Luke, his being here today would have been just too close for comfort. With so much heartache from the past year on her mind, the last thing she needed was to relive her romance—and breakup—with Luke Hunter.

Banners advertising the surf camp whipped in the breeze. By the time Maggie reached check-in, Eva had already gotten her camp swag and bounded over to meet the other campers. Her daughter had never met a stranger, and though that scared her to bits sometimes, a part of her felt deeply thankful. As a kid, Maggie often vacillated between speaking her mind and hiding behind her own shadow. Sometimes lately she found herself leaning toward the latter, but being a stylist had kept her from withdrawing completely.

"You can go now, Mom," Eva told her. "I'm fine."

Maggie nodded, biting back a *yeah, right*. She knew better than to say as much in front of Eva's new friends. Instead, she said, "I think I'll stay awhile." She pointed to an area outside of the action. "I'm going to sit on a towel and read for a bit before I head back and do some more painting. If you need me, I'll—"

"I won't!"

And ... she was off. Maggie shook her head, fluffed out her towel, threw her bag onto it, and plunked herself down. She opened up her e-reader to the latest novel she'd down-loaded, and within minutes, found herself lost in story, vaguely aware of the wind dying away and the onset of heat from the sun rolling into position overhead.

"Must be a good book."

Maggie's eyes snapped up, and she shaded them quickly from streaming sunlight. Luke's sideways smile greeted her, his eyes hidden behind mirrored sunglasses.

Maggie ignored his comment. "I guess you're here to check on your camp." She glanced over to where the kids were all taking a swim test. "Looks like your staff has it under control."

"I'm sure they do. Many of them have been doing this every summer for ... years."

She noted the way he glanced at her slightly when he

said *years*. Why did that bug her so much? He certainly hadn't thought of *her* over the years—why would he? Maybe he was just letting her know how much she'd missed.

That annoyed her too.

He continued. "I trust them all but it's opening day and a good excuse to be on the beach."

"Who needs an excuse?"

Luke chuckled and put a hand on his hip. "True. My daughter and I get up early every morning, and after I make us some breakfast we come out here before heading to the shop. No excuse needed."

Her eyes landed on Luke's left hand propped on his hip. He didn't wear a ring, but that was probably so he wouldn't lose it in the surf. Unless ... marriage trouble? He'd mentioned his daughter, but where was CeCe?

Maggie forced her gaze back to the shoreline. No. This was none of her business. She knew the fallout from soul-crushing rejection, from broken vows, and didn't wish that on anyone.

The truth was, Maggie had long ago forgotten about Luke, about their teen-shaped crush. Well, maybe *forgotten* was not the right word, but she'd buried the memory all right. She'd had to, really.

She had grown up a lot in the last decade, having learned the hard way that love was much more than moony gazes at a cute boy, and that sex didn't automatically mean love. She reminded herself that the only reason her memories seemed to tower over her at the moment was because of Luke's sudden presence.

Luke motioned with his chin toward the sand beside her. "May I sit?"

She shrugged.

Apparently, he took that as a yes and settled onto the sand beside her, his knees pointing toward the sun, his arms relaxed across them. He swung a look at her, his gaze sliding slowly to the bag at her side. She noticed a thin scar above his lip that hadn't been there before. "You still a vegetarian?"

Her mind thought of her teenaged past when she was trying to save the world one cow at a time. "Not in years."

Luke shrank back, obviously surprised.

She frowned. "What?"

"You were pretty vocal about it back then. Shamed a lot of guys who ate burgers after a session."

Maggie rolled her gaze upward, though she knew he was right. Thing was, she'd also forgotten all about her teenaged love affair with vegetarianism. One thing she had not forgotten, though, was how displeased her mother was about her food choices. Once, frustrated by her daughter's constant criticism of the daily menu, her mother had suggested that Maggie just "go graze out on the lawn!"

Pretty hard to do when surrounded by sand.

Maggie's ex-husband, Greg, loved beef, so she had learned to cook it, often with fancy vegetables and salads to satisfy that yearning within her for something healthy to go alongside. But after he left and Eva began to turn up her cute little nose at Maggie's attempts at gourmet foods, she gave up. Soon mac and cheese and hamburgers or chicken or hot dogs—accentuated with a carrot stick or two—had become the mainstay in her kitchen.

"Well, I'm sure they survived." She paused. "Unless they didn't from all that, you know, cholesterol."

"Ha. Right."

Luke relaxed back on his elbows, revealing his flat abdomen and long, muscular legs. Other than vague crow's-feet that appeared when he squinted out to sea, it was as if nothing had changed. She turned away. He was still the guy who had caught her heart every summer when her family would land in Colibri at the beginning of the season. Only he'd aged, in a good way.

Some things weren't fair.

Especially since she wasn't sure if she could exactly say the same for herself.

Maggie's mind wandered back to her ten-year high school reunion a couple of years ago. The event had revealed former football players with beer guts and heartthrobs with bad attitudes and the inability to age well. She'd run into plenty of thirty-year-olds who looked closer to forty and beyond.

But Luke? Somehow over the years since she'd been gone, he had moved from a wiry boy they all called *String-bean*, to a thick-muscled, wholly ripened man. She half-expected him to turn over onto his side and spear her with those gray-blue eyes of his.

Maggie forced her gaze away. She had a book to read and a kid to look out for—where was she again?

She craned her neck and spotted Eva right away. Her daughter had already proven her swimming ability—something Maggie had prided herself on—and was goofing around with several new friends who waited on the shore for the next phase of camp.

"So I'm guessing that's not a salad in your bag then."

"Are you hungry or something?" Maggie grabbed her

bag, dragging it over to her lap. "I'm getting the idea that you didn't manage breakfast this morning."

Luke chuckled. "No, thanks. I'm good."

"Then why the interest in my eating habits?" She wanted to add: *We haven't seen each other in years and this is all you can think of to talk about?*

"Just making conversation."

"Hm."

He quieted now, the crush of waves tossing up memories that she'd hoped would get pulled back out with the tide. She didn't want this to feel commonplace or normal. Several times she darted a glance around, expecting to see CeCe show up, looking like she had walked out of a fashion blog.

And their child. A daughter, she'd heard, though Maggie had worked hard at not learning too much more than that.

She frowned, biting the inside of her lip. Sitting here with Luke, watching her child—their child—felt all too wrong. Her stomach roiled enough that she thought she might be sick.

"You all right? Not worrying about Eva, I hope. My staff members are all great teachers, if that's what's got you looking like you had a bad bite of sushi."

His voice was teasing. He always did like to tease, but she would not be falling for it this time. Or ever again. Some things were not worth repeating.

Maggie sucked in a breath, settling her stomach the best she could. She changed the subject. "Looks like a pretty big surf event coming to Colibri next month. Will tents be pitched on the sand or ...?"

Luke exhaled. "I'd forgotten all about the way things

used to run around here. In answer to your question, not likely."

"Really?"

"Town's trying to keep the homeless from camping on the beaches, so they've outlawed it for everyone."

"I see."

He sighed. "So people have been opening up their homes, renting rooms or whole houses for the event."

"Makes sense."

Luke wagged his head. "Yes and no, especially if you're against vacation rentals, which many of the locals are."

"Wow. It's all more complicated than I thought." She quieted a moment, wisps of her hair blowing on the breeze. Gratitude for a subject change filled her.

"Complicated is an understatement."

Didn't she know it. "Well," she finally said, "my dad was never that crazy about seeing all those campers in front of our beach house, but my sisters and I thought it was fun."

Luke coughed out a surprised laugh. "You were flirts."

She snapped a look at him, expecting to see accusation in his expression. Instead, his eyes danced.

She licked her lips, thinking. "Untrue. We were just ... curious."

"Ha. Right. Curious flirts. And your mom was an accomplice."

Maggie shrank back.

Luke quirked that crooked smile at her again, and it sent a weird chill of a ripple through her.

She forced her gaze away from his face. "No idea what you're talking about."

"All I can say is sending you all out with baskets of cookies was brilliant."

Maggie swallowed, suddenly remembering a side of her mother she had not thought of in a long while. She liked to bake. And to laugh. And mostly, to share. Luke was ... right. When scores of surfers showed up for events in the summer, camping right out on their beach, she would scoot her and her sisters outside to distribute cookies. She kind of recalled Jake hovering, as if for protection.

She slid a glance at Luke. "Okay. I'm beginning to remember that. My mom had a good and giving heart, but, well, let me just say that I'd never send Eva into a den of surfers with a bunch of cookies!"

Luke leaned back and laughed, the sound of it hearty and oddly high-pitched. He lifted his chin again and wagged his head, smiling. "That's the Maggie I knew."

Once again, Maggie pulled her chin away from Luke's gaze. She wasn't a kid anymore and didn't believe in holding grudges, but time had not healed her wounded heart completely, at least not enough to fall back into her old ways. And especially not with a former, married crush.

Luke pulled himself up, a light dusting of sand knocking across her feet. He looked down. "They're getting ready to do some board work. I'm going to go talk to the staff. Any message you'd like me to give Eva?"

Maggie scoffed. "Not if I want to keep my good mom card."

He grinned. "Understood." He paused. "Listen, I have to get back to the shop. Good catching up with you, Maggie."

"Hm, yes. You as well." She gave him the most non-committal wave as he headed down closer to the water.

Thankfully, he hadn't shown up here in his bare feet, wearing a wetsuit and carrying his board. She was long over him now, but did she have to be reminded of the surfer he once was and how he always could make her swoon just by showing up?

No. Positively no. Maggie dragged in a breath and allowed it to roll through her slowly, oxygen offering her relief. She had weathered her first test and passed. She and Eva would likely be gone from Colibri Beach when the surf competition came to town, and for that, Maggie was grateful. Otherwise, she would be subjected to women throwing themselves at Luke like they had a dozen years ago.

That was something she never, ever wanted to see again.

3

Maggie shimmied her feet deeper into the sand as she twisted her hair into a pom-pom on her head. Her phone rang and she groaned, dropping her twist of hair. "Hey, Daisy," she said.

"Maggie, I'm so sorry, but I'm going to have to change my mom's hair appointment."

She sat up straight. "Everything all right?"

"She's still asleep. Guess Jake and I kept her up too late, you know, talking and all."

"You mean making out like a couple of teenagers."

Daisy giggled. "You could say that."

Maggie smiled. Her brother drove her crazy when they were kids, but she was happy for him. He and his generous heart deserved love and she couldn't think of a better person than Daisy Mcafee to join their family. A ripple of sadness fluttered through her, a wish that she could find something similar in her life, someone to talk to, to parent with, but she chased the feeling away like a rogue wave.

"So, anyway," Daisy continued, "is there any way we could reschedule for tomorrow?"

"Absolutely. I'll be there."

She'd barely disconnected the call when her phone rang again. Maggie frowned. She didn't recognize the number, but it was coming from her town in Arizona. "Hello?"

"Maggie Holloway? This is Cassandra, owner of Marshmallow."

Marshmallow was the name of the most sought-after salon back home. "Oh! Thank you for calling me back."

"How can I help you?"

"Well, I'm looking to make a change." No need to mention the situation was quickly becoming dire. "I'm hoping you have a chair available?"

"Normally, I would say no, but as a matter of fact, one has opened up. Are you interested in applying for it?"

Maggie glanced out to the sea, its surface glimmering. She couldn't stay here forever, tempting as the thought of seeing those waves every day might be. Eventually, the family beach house would be sold and Maggie would receive her portion, but until then—and beyond, really—she needed to make a living.

Except for family members scattered about, everything and everyone Eva knew was in Arizona, so moving back there was the logical choice. If only she had been able to pay her rent, she would have somewhere to land when they returned. Maggie brushed away that sad thought and instead asked for the cost of a weekly chair rental at Marshmallow.

A moment later, she hung up. The welcome sunlight had turned hot on her skin and she had to wrap her towel around her for shade. Unfortunately, that only made her sweat. Maggie blew out a sigh, her conversation with Cassandra replaying in her mind.

No way could she afford such a high chair rental!

Not unless she had a slew of customers to bring with her. Oh, she had some, but her old salon shut down abruptly. It was in a touristy area, which meant not a lot of regulars. And then the bills piled up and she found herself unable to pay them all.

Shame filled her face and she bit back tears. Jake had been so, so good to her, even though her pride kept her from asking for the help she needed. If it were not for him, she had no idea where she and Eva might have ended up, but oh how she wanted to break out of the cycle of lack. Maggie so wanted to teach her daughter the value of independence.

A flash of a football flying caught in her gaze. Maggie squinted. Up ahead, a rugged guy with dark hair and a deep tan leaped upward and caught the ball, hugged it to himself, then landed hard on the ground.

Rafael.

Jake had mentioned that Colibri Beach's resident heartbreaker was still around. Apparently, he'd gotten a little too close to Daisy last month, much to Jake's annoyance. Maggie didn't care to let her brother know about her own encounter with the sexy Rafael ...

She watched as Rafael rolled into a standing position as if he had hardly grazed the ground, and then hold the ball into the air with one strong arm. The move, not to mention Rafael's dark and brooding looks, took her back to when she had first run home to Greg. She had just had her heart broken in two by Luke and there Greg was, standing on the stoop of their apartment building, looking as if had been waiting just for her. He had always been her fallback and she his, and this time, the timing aligned. Greg swept up the dust of her crumbled heart, and for a time, she thought their union could last.

Maggie bit her lip and looked across the divide to where a lithe blonde, hair billowing behind her, laughed as if Rafael's move was the coolest thing she had ever seen.

Some things never changed.

"Mom!"

Maggie snapped her gaze away from Rafael and his latest conquest to where her daughter stood out among the crowd of newbie surfers. They all wore wetsuits, but she recognized Eva immediately by the way she continually bounced on her toes. "Ready?" she called.

Eva nodded and Maggie joined her quickly.

Her daughter scrunched her face. "Were you here the whole time?"

"You bet I was."

Eva sighed, dramatically. "You shoulda gone and done mom things."

Maggie tilted her head, a smile emerging. "Oh, yeah? What kind of mom things?" The thought of a mani-pedi tempted her deeply.

Eva shrugged. "Like laundry or making me lunch. Stuff like that."

Maggie frowned. *Those were mom things?*

Eva cracked up.

Maggie dipped a look at her. "You think that's funny, huh?"

Eva nodded. "Yup."

Maggie reached into her bag and pulled out a wet-dry brush and a bottle of detangler. "Well, then, just you wait!"

Eva squealed and began sprinting toward home. With a laugh and a shake of her head, Maggie tossed her torture products into her bag and followed after her daughter, grateful not to run into Luke again.

THE NEXT MORNING, Luke scrolled up and down the spreadsheet in front of him, thankful for good advice. If Maggie's father hadn't offered him some when he was making money faster than he knew how to handle it, he doubted there would be much left now. Thankfully, though, he had managed to buy this building and stow away some savings for the lean times, which, by the looks of it, equaled right about now.

Good thing the summer season was about to kick in.

He glanced at the time. Regardless of having plenty of work to do, Luke needed to leave now if he was going to catch the end of surf camp for the day. Having a camp with his name on it was his way of blowing raspberries at his fears. He might have hung up surfing, but he recognized how knowing the art of balance and patience would benefit the kids out there.

On his way out of the shop, Luke glanced up at the bare spot on his wall—the reason he had missed yesterday's camp closing. He sighed. The longboard that had hung there, one that he had torn up the waves with many times, was someone else's adventure to ride now. He gave the empty wall one last lingering look and headed out the door.

When Luke arrived at camp, he scanned the beach. Maggie stood closer to the action today, shading her eyes from the sun. For some reason that he couldn't explain, Luke lingered near the street, watching her. If he closed his eyes for a few seconds, he could hear her voice in his head ... feel the smile on her lips ... smell the sugar from her kiss.

Honk!

Startled, Luke turned to see a couple of old-timers trying to pull into the spot that he was occupying.

"Get outta my space," one of them called. "We've gotta board meeting to get to!"

Luke grimaced and shook his head. *Pull yourself together.* He hopped up on the curb, threw out a wave to the guys, and headed toward the water. Maggie had not moved by the time he joined her. "How's Eva liking camp?"

She spun around, a splash of her Perrier landing on his arm. Maggie bit her lip. "Sorry about that."

He chuckled. "I'm the one who should apologize."

She frowned.

"For startling you."

"Hm. Okay." Maggie looked out to where a dozen or so young surfers clung to boards, most of them on their knees. "It's scarier than I remembered."

He brushed his gaze over her, noting how well a decade looked on her. "For Eva ... or for you?"

Maggie sighed, noticeably. "Eva's not afraid of anything. I'm the one who could barely sleep last night."

"Really? Why's that?"

"Well, it's one thing for them to pretend they're surfing while safely on the sand. But it's another entirely to send your baby out into that treacherous sea."

In his gut, Luke knew he should assure Maggie that Eva was perfectly fine. He ran a surf shop ... shaped boards for a living. Not to mention, his name was on the surf camp, and he had a piece of himself riding out there as well. His head told him that surfing was not only safe but a great workout for both the body and the mind.

But that same old gut-clenching began the minute he opened his mouth. So he clamped his mouth shut.

"I'm surprised you're not out there," she said, suddenly.

Her voice pulled him back to reality. "What was that?"

Maggie turned and looked more fully at him than she had since the day they had run into each other at the shop. She tilted her head the way she always had, scrutinizing him. "How often do you surf these days, Luke?"

Luke's gaze washed over the eyes that stared up at him. They were brown and lush and he wanted to tell her the truth. But could he? She still had those freckles across the bridge of her nose, still needled her bottom lip as she waited for him to respond. Always patient. Why hadn't he appreciated that about her more?

"I hung it up."

She tilted her head farther. "Hung up what?"

He swung his gaze to the sea, to the newbie surfers learning the sport under his company's banner, then back to those loam-colored eyes of hers. It was as if time had halted. He was barely twenty again and she ... the love of his life. Luke swallowed his dread of answering her question. "I stopped surfing years ago, Maggie."

"I don't believe you."

Her expression told him that was true. He'd broken her trust years ago, and though her sudden appearance after so many years away had prickled his hope—of what, he wasn't certain—he knew she was telling the truth. She saw him as the same guy she had left. A jerk who surfed.

Luke crossed his arms in front of his body. "Surfing is a rush. I love watching it and I suspect that I always will. But, I'm done." He looked down at the toe of his flip-flop as he stabbed it into the sand. "Wasn't all it was cracked up to be," he said, quietly.

"You're serious."

"I am."

"And the women? Were they all they were cracked up to be?"

Her tone had turned biting, and it stung. But he had changed. He believed they both had. Luke's jaw clicked and he licked his lips, ready with a retort.

"Luke?" A young woman in a wetsuit called out to him. Tara. One of the surf camp staffers he had hired. He could almost feel Maggie's *I told you so* gaze burning into him.

He held his expression in check and turned his attention to his employee. "Yes?"

"We're running over. Some of the kids aren't done with the drills. Is that okay?"

He began to nod when Maggie spoke up. "Actually, I need to get going because I have an appointment. Is Eva finished?"

Before Tara could answer, Luke said, "I'm happy to keep an eye on her for you. I can bring her by the house later."

"I couldn't ask that."

"It's not a problem. She and Siena can get to know each other better."

"Siena?"

"My daughter." He swiveled a look out to the campers, pointing. "She's ... well, she's actually standing on the other side of Eva right now. I've heard they're already becoming friends."

Maggie didn't answer. A confused expression crossed her face, followed by something he could not exactly name. Fear, maybe. Did she not trust him? True, he hadn't exactly let things end well, but that was years ago and they were standing here as adults. Full-fledged parents. Surely she knew he could be trusted with her daughter. Especially since he was a father himself.

Abruptly, she moved past him, sand kicking behind her. "No. Thanks anyway. She's done with the course, so I'll grab her now and head home."

4

His daughter. Of course. How could she forget—or in this case, put aside—the fact that Luke had a child? And a ... wife.

Maggie continued to massage shampoo into Wren's hair, her mind fixated on the fact that Eva and Siena had spent the past few days of surf camp together like old pals, while she had nearly forgotten the child's existence. A pang of guilt stabbed at her, her own secret weighing on her. Until now, the truth she kept hidden, that nobody but her mother and Greg—and God—knew about began to gnaw at her.

She hadn't intended to hurt anyone. That fact alone was why she had prayed so hard in those early years, and why she had kept the truth hidden all these years—to not disrupt any more lives.

Maggie bit back a pained sigh. She had to focus on what was in front of her and not on the past. She flipped a look at Wren. Though her client was nearly asleep, Maggie had learned long ago that she felt most at peace when working.

Yesterday, she dashed to the next town over and picked up an inflatable hair washing station from a salon supply store. After rinsing Wren's hair with water from a pitcher, Maggie massaged conditioner into her otherwise dry, gray locks, but the woman's eyes kept lolling shut.

Oh to be that relaxed ... ever.

For the next half hour or so, Maggie put aside her worries. She clipped, dried, and styled Wren's hair, often having to help her stay awake in the process. By the time she was done, the elderly woman's eyes shone.

"I look beautiful!"

Maggie squeezed the woman's shoulders in a hug. "You absolutely do, Wren." She smacked a kiss on Wren's cheek. "Can I do anything else for you before I go?"

"You have already done more than you know! Your mother would be so proud of you, Maggie."

An hour later, as Maggie rolled another swath of paint on the downstairs bathroom wall, she thought about what Wren said about her mother being proud of her. She twisted her lips, the thought of those words bringing an old ache to her heart. Her parents had gone out to Arizona to visit many times, always showering Eva with love, but Maggie often found herself unable to look them in the eyes. It was as if her failings might mirror back to her.

Was that selfish? To justify pushing her parents away because of her own feelings of inadequacy and failure?

"Mom?"

Eva's voice snapped Maggie to the present.

"Hm?"

"How come you're painting over the mirror?"

Maggie frowned. Slowly, she swiveled her gaze back to

where she had been working and her daughter was right: She had painted right over the edge of the mirror. The brand new mirror that Jake had installed. She sighed and grabbed a rag.

"So anyway," Eva continued, "I was thinking that maybe I should get another swimsuit."

Maggie scrubbed harder, biting back a laugh.

"What's so funny?" Eva's impish face wore a confused expression, her forehead scrunched.

"You," Maggie said, pretending to dot Eva's face with a paintbrush. "*You're* so funny. One minute you're telling me I messed up, and the next, you're talking about swimwear."

"Oh." Eva batted her eyes. "Does that mean we can go shopping?"

Maggie sighed and leaned against the bathroom counter. She didn't have the money for this, but then again, how long would that old suit of Eva's hold up underneath a wetsuit with daily surfing lessons in that salt-laden water? "Fine. Give me a half hour to clean up and then we'll go."

Eva shot a fist into the air. "Yes!"

An hour or so later, Maggie and Eva wound up at Brooke's Bakery for an afternoon snack.

"Looks like you two have been shopping," Lea said, pointing at the bag in Eva's hand.

Eva bounced up on her toes. "I needed another one 'cause the one I had was wearing out."

Maggie hooked a tendril of Eva's hair behind her ear. "I'm rewarding her for the fact that it took her all of ten minutes to pick one out."

Lea gasped. The pony-tailed woman came around the

counter to high-five Eva. "Wow. You're my inspiration," she said with a laugh.

Maggie laughed too. "Seriously."

Lea was still smiling when she went back around the counter. "What can I get you ladies?"

Eva asked for an eclair, while Maggie opted for a cinnamon-and-sugar muffin top and a cup of coffee to go.

After Maggie had paid, Lea said, "I've been meaning to call you about my hair, but I know you've been busy."

"I'm happy to make time for you."

"I appreciate that, girl!" Lea wagged her head slowly, as the bakery's front door dinged. "You sure have had a lot on your plate, what with painting, and surf camp, and doing Wren's hair."

Maggie nearly spit out her sip of coffee. She swallowed it back and tilted her head to one side. "Is my schedule posted on the internet somewhere?"

Lea wrinkled her brow before dawning came over her. "That's funny." She batted the air with a hand as if knowing Maggie's daily schedule was a given. "Word travels around here, you know."

"So," Maggie said, "would you like to come by tomorrow after lunch? I can do your hair in our guest bath, if you don't mind that I'm still painting it."

"Aw, really? That would be so great but I promised Brooke I'd work the afternoon shift for her."

Maggie slid to the side, aware that someone had stepped up to the counter. She thought for a second. "What time are you done here?"

A familiar voice cut in. "Excuse me," Luke said. "I didn't mean to eavesdrop, but if you're busy tomorrow,

Siena and I would be happy to bring Eva to and from camp."

Eva spoke up. "That would be fun! Can I, Mom?"

A sheet of ice formed inside Maggie. Luke stood there, waiting for her answer, being kind as could be, and another piece of her insides tore away. "Oh, I don't know—"

"C'mon, Momma, please?"

Maggie's mind spun as her daughter jostled next to her with that impish expression on her face. At home, she wasn't used to so much help. Maggie usually had to barter for Eva's rides, and sometimes even beg a little. If her mother hadn't flown to Arizona to help her through her postpartum depression after Eva was born and the sudden defection of her husband, she might not have survived.

She pulled her mind to the present. If only things had not been as they were ... if only ...

Eva continued to tilt her chin up. "Please?"

It was only a couple of rides, rides that would take all of five minutes. Six, tops. Greg was never helpful with things like that, even before the baby was born. And when he had decided that marriage and parenting weren't for him—even though he knew her secret and had wooed her anyway—he walked away from them both, as if they had never even existed.

In some ways, it reminded her of the way Luke had walked away from her once, too.

Maggie glanced warily at Luke, keenly aware of the dark eyes trained on her, a question held in them. "Sure CeCe won't mind?"

An odd expression crossed his face. "No, she's—uh—well, she's not around much these days."

Maggie frowned. What did *that* mean? Then again, it wouldn't be surprising to learn that a surf shop in this small town couldn't exactly pay all the bills. Of course, CeCe worked somewhere. Probably had an enviable career of some sort.

When she didn't reply, Luke added, "Honestly, Mags. I don't mind at all."

He watched her in earnest, his brows knit together, that dimple in his chin becoming increasingly unavoidable. *You're a lucky girl, CeCe ...*

"Okay," she said. "I guess that would be fine. Thank you."

Eva squealed.

Maggie turned to Lea. "Well, it appears that my morning suddenly opened up."

"Hooray! Should I come by around ten?"

"Perfect." Maggie turned to leave, aware that a line had formed, though by the unwavering way Luke's eyes were trained on her, he didn't seem to have noticed. "Thanks, again."

As Maggie brushed past him, Luke tapped her on the shoulder. She lifted her chin, their gazes colliding. "My pleasure."

"You're a miracle worker."

Maggie laughed at Lea's compliment. In her experience, women were usually on a high after having their hair done. Time would tell if her new friend would still think the same of her skills a few days from now.

"Seriously, Maggie, this has been the most fun I've had in

ages." Lea sighed. "Unfortunately, I have to work sixty hours a week just to make enough to live, let alone have fun."

"I hear you. Rent's not cheap."

Lea turned around. "Any thought of keeping this place? Then we could be neighbors and you could do my hair for me all the time!"

Maggie smiled. "Sadly, no." She sighed, looking at Lea in the mirror. "Fact is, I'm without a chair at the moment, so as soon as Eva and I leave here, we're heading into the great unknown."

"Why go back then?" Lea paused. "Oh. Is it because of a custody issue?"

"Custody?"

"Eva's father. You know, do you have to stay in Arizona?"

Maggie unplugged the flat iron, pretending to be distracted. She didn't care to speak about Greg to anyone. He'd lied to her recently when she had given him credit for the financial help she thought he was giving her. It had been a surprise, given his sudden about-face so soon after they married. As it turned out, Jake had been the one secretly depositing money into her bank account ...

The last brawl she had with her ex-husband was too raw, too biting. She'd not ever shared it with anyone, and if she could manage to keep her mouth shut the next few weeks, she never would.

Slowly, she said, "Something like that. But really, Eva's friends are there, and it's the only hometown she's ever known."

"Well, I don't know about that. She seems to have taken to Colibri really well if you ask me. I know you guys were only around in the summers—"

"And sometimes during the year, when work was slow for my dad." Maggie didn't mention to Lea all of it—that they had lost their family home in a fire. After that tragedy, the beach house had become even more important to her parents. Unfortunately, her father could never quite dig up enough work here for them to put down deep roots. So for a time, they had become nomads of sorts.

Lea nodded her head. "That's right. I think I remember seeing you at other times of the year, too. All I meant was that, well, kids are so adaptable, you know? And Eva looks right at home here. So, if you ever change your mind about moving here for good, I'd love to be her auntie."

LATER, Maggie was still thinking about her conversation with Lea as she cleaned up the bathroom-turned-salon and waited for Eva to arrive home. She grabbed a paint brush and touched up an area around the new bathtub she had missed. Her new-old friend was right—Eva did seem fairly happy here. And why not? No school, a big old beach out there, and nothing but time to spend. Maybe it was Maggie who couldn't see herself living here, the heap of memories too tall to conquer.

When her phone rang, she snatched it up, concerned about the time. "Hello?"

"Maggie?" Luke's voice greeted her, mingled with the high-pitched laughter of girls talking over one another. "So, remember the ice cream place up the block from my shop? The one that's only open in summer?"

"Yes." She hadn't thought of that place in years.

"We're on our way there now to celebrate the end of surf camp for the day." The girls squealed louder and Luke raised his voice. "Join us?"

"Yeah, Mom!" Eva called out. "Come with us!"

Maggie frowned. He was supposed to drop her off at home after camp, not take any detours. What if she didn't want Eva to have ice cream before lunch? *Or what if she didn't want to spend any more time with Luke Hunter than she had to ...*

Then again, she knew how persuasive little girls could be. She pictured the impish pout Eva had mastered and suspected that Siena had dropped her own version of one on Luke. Dads were so gullible sometimes. The good ones, anyway. Her stomach sank a little at what they'd lost, at what could never be ...

"So you'll join us?" Luke interrupted her thoughts, prompting her to waver.

Her mind shifted again to Luke's wife. What would CeCe's reaction be if she showed up to join Luke and the girls for ice cream like she was participating in some cozy family outing? She shuddered at the idea of running into Luke's wife again after so many years. They weren't friends back then, for obvious reasons, but high school was over, right? Surely the two of them could be adults. They had to be, for their children's sake.

Then again ... he had said something cryptic about her. What was it again? Just as she had gained some courage, she lost it again. Maybe she should tell them no, absolutely not. Although, a scoop of something was tempting right now ...

"Momma, are you coming?"

"Hear that, Mags?" Luke was saying, coaxing her to join them.

She sighed. How often does a young daughter want to spend time in public with her mother? And exactly how many more years would that last?

If she used her own teen years as an example, not long. "Okay. Sure," she said. "I'll meet you there."

MAGGIE WOULD NEVER FORGET the smell of old sugar in the creamery. How could she? It was one of the first places she and her siblings would run to after they rolled into Colibri Beach each summer. Well, after they'd emptied their suitcases and put away their clothes neatly. "First things first," their mother always admonished when they first walked into the beach house.

Maggie entered the creamery and, two steps in, her flip-flops were already sticking to the floor. Another memory. Fortunately, the shop shined everywhere else with its seasonal fresh coat of white paint on the walls and gleaming lights over the single case of ice cream flavors, and for a quick second, the lack of change calmed Maggie's nerves.

Eva waved at her from a twisted iron-backed chair at the far end of the shop. Luke sat across from her, and the girl standing next to him with an arm propped on his shoulder, she guessed, was Siena. She froze. Though older than Eva, Sienna was a wisp of a girl who appeared much younger than her age. Her yellow-blonde hair was held back by a headband, and if Maggie had not known her mother's identity already, she would have been able to guess.

Siena looked like a miniature version of CeCe.

Luke craned a look toward the door and flashed her a smile.

Maggie sucked in a breath and approached the group. "I thought you were all coming here for ice cream."

"We are!" Siena said.

Luke's expression had sobered. He put his hand on his daughter's back. "Siena, I'd like you to meet a friend of mine. This is Eva's mother, Maggie."

Siena waved. "Hi."

Eva cut in. "Can we get ice cream now?"

Luke tilted his head. "I told them we had to wait for you."

Maggie smiled at Siena, who seemed genuinely smitten with her father. "It is nice to meet you, Siena." She turned to Eva. "Be patient, you."

Eva and Siena took off to the ice cream case and Luke stood. He gestured to his own nose. "You, uh, you have paint on your, uh ..."

Maggie ran her fingers over her nose and peeled paint right off of it. "Oops. Sorry. After Lea left, I decided to do some touch-up. That's what I was doing when you called."

He grinned. "So you've been busy all morning. Sounds like you needed this break."

Maggie felt her expression cloud. For a quick second, everything about this moment felt normal. Just a couple of friends and their kids grabbing an ice cream cone. And in some ways, the last ten years had spun by like a blur. She wanted to harness all the good times, such as watching her sweet daughter grow up spunky and kind, but the angst of lost love and financial and career hardships was something she preferred to bury deep in the sand.

"Mom, can I have two scoops?"

Maggie rolled her eyes and followed Luke over to the case. Siena had already been served up a fat scoop of something pink and unappetizing-looking. Maggie put her hands on her daughter's shoulders. "Just one'll do."

Eva scrunched her nose and looked to the girl behind the case wearing a hat and holding an ice cream scoop. "I'll have pistachio."

"Good choice," Luke said.

He gestured to Maggie to order, but she shook her head. "No, thanks." She had cringed when passing the bakery on the way over here and realized she'd already been in that pink creampuff of a place twice this week. Maybe a scoop of something wasn't the best idea.

Luke frowned playfully, but shrugged and looked to the server. "Okay, then, make that two scoops of pistachio."

Eva gasped a little and Luke laughed. "I meant one for her and one for me."

Maggie's gaze caught on a lone gallon of frozen yogurt. She gestured toward it. "That any good?"

The server turned up both palms, including the one holding an ice cream scoop. "Moms like it, so I guess so."

She bit her lip, resigned. "Okay. I'll have a scoop of that, but in a cup."

When she went for her purse, Luke held up a hand like a stop sign. "I've got this."

Maggie shook her head. "No, that's—"

Luke whipped out a bill and handed it to the waiting cashier. He dipped a look at Maggie. "I invited you. Remember?"

She let her purse swing out of her hand and took the cup from the young woman who had served them. Luke leaned toward her as they walked back to the table. "They're best friends already."

Maggie froze. The two girls sat, their heads tilted toward each other as they simultaneously ate their ice creams and talked about who-knew-what ... like sisters. Unease slithered through Maggie.

Luke stepped in front of her, his back to the girls. He spoke quietly. "You okay?"

She snapped a look at him, a sudden memory showering down on her like ice. "Why wouldn't I be?"

Luke's expression sobered. He took a bite of his ice cream, watching her.

Maggie huffed out a sigh and let her gaze wander across the shop where kids huddled together around summer's favorite pastime. Why couldn't she just relax and let the moment be? So what if she and Eva would be leaving soon? Maggie and her siblings had done this very thing for years— visit Colibri for a brief time—and it hadn't scarred them for life or anything.

Of course, she had never made a bestie in her mother's ex-boyfriend's daughter, the one whose existence precipitated their breakup.

Even to her, that was a mouthful.

Maggie rolled a look up at Luke who ate his ice cream in silence. Quietly, she asked, "How does CeCe feel about me being here?"

His expression went stony. "She wouldn't care, Maggie."

"I doubt that."

"Why do you say that?"

Maggie tipped her chin up. "Just being honest with you. We were never friends, Jake."

He seemed to consider that, yet said nothing to confirm or deny what she'd said. Instead, "And like I said, she doesn't care what I do, who I'm friends with ..."

"What do you mean? Doesn't she know that I'm here?"—she lowered her voice—"That Eva's here? Because I don't feel right hanging out with a married man—"

"I'm not married."

Maggie searched his face. She saw no hurt there, but instead, a kind of steely resolve. "I-I didn't know." She looked down into her cup. "How long have you been divorced?"

"I'm not."

She snapped a look up, her voice quieter still. "You mean, CeCe, um—"

"She's not dead, if that's what you're thinking." Something harsh flared in Luke's expression. As quick as it appeared, it left him and she knew this was something he didn't care to talk about. But she pressed on. "Then why did you say you aren't married?"

"Because CeCe left us a long time ago."

"Oh. So, she's gone? How-how does that work for Siena?"

His voice quieted into a whisper. "CeCe is an addict, Mags."

Maggie covered her mouth with her hand.

"The divorce is just a formality," he said, softly. "She asked for it, and so I relented, but she hasn't been much help lately."

Maggie nodded, a million questions in her head, most that she would never ask. Finally, though, she asked, "Does Siena live with you full-time?"

Instead of an edge, a downcast look rolled through Luke's features. "Yes, she does."

Maggie stole a look at the girl with the flyaway hair who looked just like her mother. Without all the *Mean Girls*-type drama, that is. She lifted her gaze back to Luke. "We should probably talk sometime when it's less ... public."

He licked the pistachio ice cream from his lips. "I think I can handle that."

"Good."

Luke flashed a sad little smile then and led them both to the table. The girls were in full chatter mode, and Maggie nearly felt short of breath.

"Hey, Mom?" Eva said, loudly. "Why didn't the beagle want to go to the beach?"

Maggie scrunched her mouth, her mind struggling to move from heavy thoughts to those that were far lighter. But she tried. "Hmm. It wanted to stay home and sleep?"

"No. It didn't want to be a hot dog."

Maggie smiled, grateful for the freeing feeling of it.

Siena looked at her. "Maggie, do you know what the beach said to the surfer?"

"I'm really not sure."

"Nothing! It just waved!"

Luke threw back his head and let loose that deranged laugh of his, which cracked Maggie up. When the laughter quieted between them, Luke said, "You always were a good listener."

"Thanks, although I'm not sure my parents would have always agreed with that."

Luke glanced at the girls, who had fallen back into their own conversation. "Yes, well, parents have a lot to compete with." He winked at her. "Seriously, I bet that listening ear of yours has served you well as a hairstylist."

"Yes, I suppose it has." She fiddled with the spoon in her cup, but didn't take a bite. Those persistent questions hung on the edge of her tongue, but she pushed them away. Instead, she asked, "How about your job? Do you have someone watching the shop for you?"

"I do. A couple of avid surfers come in several times a week. Pay isn't great, but the discounts are."

"I'm sure that goes a long way."

He leaned forward, grinning, but before Luke could say a thing, a woman's voice broke into the conversation.

"Well, well, well, look at all of you together!"

All four chins turned toward the woman who had joined their circle. Lillian Madsen, the town's most notorious realtor, stood there looking highly bejeweled and smugly happy with herself.

"If I did not know better, I'd say that you looked like one happy family sitting here."

Luke's expression was a mask. "Hello, Lillian."

The woman nodded, her Cheshire-cat smile growing longer still. "Luke." She turned to Maggie, a sad pout suddenly appearing on her face. "Dear Maggie. I was so terribly sorry to hear about your parents' accident. Such a tragedy. How are you doing, dear?"

"We are all managing very well. Thank you." Maggie hoped her answer was enough to make the vulture fly off to her cave. She had been warned by her siblings that Lillian would show some sort of sympathy, but that the woman was really only after one thing: her family's beach house listing. The woman had no shame—she'd even tried to talk Daisy into selling her mother's home while Wren was still in the hospital after her stroke.

Lillian nodded, a heavy frown pulling at the corners of her lipstick-layered mouth. "That's good to hear." She presented a card as if it were a sleight of hand trick. "I understand that you and your siblings are hard at work improving the beach house. I am here to list it for you, when you need me."

Maggie took the card and tucked it into the pocket of her hoodie without looking at it. "I'll keep you in mind."

Lillian wasn't deterred. "Perhaps we can meet this week, say, tomorrow at ten a.m.?"

Luke spoke up. "That won't work. I need her at surf camp. She has your card, Lillian. I'm sure she'll call you if your services become necessary."

Lillian pooched her lips tightly, the lines in her upper lip deepening dramatically. She thrust her chin forward, her brows raised. "You mean *when* they become necessary, Luke." She winked at Maggie and mouthed *call me* before turning on her shiny black heels and leaving them alone.

Maggie owed Luke one. He had managed to get rid of that pesky real estate agent without being rude. Her family had warned her about the woman, but she had not prepared herself for the woman's lack of manners masquerading as concern. Shew! That woman offered up condolences and a contract in nearly the same breath.

When the girls were finished with their ice cream, Maggie said, "Thanks again for picking up Eva. I appreciate it." She turned her attention to her daughter. "Ready to go and get some real food in you?"

Eva shrugged. "I guess." She and Siena walked on ahead of them.

When they reached the door, Luke held it open for

Maggie. "Speaking of real food, I'd like to take you to dinner tonight. Go with me?"

His sudden invitation stopped her. Not more than ten minutes earlier, Maggie thought Luke was a married man. Well, he sort of still was, and that truth alone left lingering questions and warnings. Maggie blocked the doorway now, her mind a tangle of thoughts.

"Excuse me." A woman and her toddler were attempting to enter so Maggie slid out of their way, bumping into Luke as she did. He caught her, his warm hand settling on her lower back. She flicked him a quick smile and continued through the doorway and out onto the sidewalk. Luke's hand found her side, and he touched her briefly. She spun around.

"So. Dinner tonight?"

Maggie licked her lips, thinking. She glanced at Eva, who continued to chatter with Siena near Luke's car.

Luke shoved his hands into his pockets, his warm expression cooling some. "I thought maybe we could have that talk you mentioned earlier."

"Yes. Sure. I'll check to see if Eva can hang out with Daisy tonight."

He grinned. "Great. I'll pick you up at six."

5

Maggie stood back, admiring a job well done. She had just finished applying a coat of paint in the large first-floor bathroom, which, unfortunately, included more than one dollop of drying paint on her sweats. As her eyes roamed around the room, checking the corners, she became vaguely aware of girlish chatter coming from Eva's room. After Luke had chased off Lillian and they all had finished their ice cream and yogurt, and after he had nudged her into saying yes to having dinner with him, the girls begged to hang out.

More than once she'd questioned her sanity.

Eva appeared in the doorway. "Mom? We're still hungry. Can we have the rest of the mac and cheese? I promise to eat the tomatoes." Her daughter flashed her a wide and fake smile.

Adding chopped tomatoes was Maggie's way of making macaroni and cheese somewhat healthy. But Eva had long ago figured out how to smoosh the tomatoes against the side of the bowl, making them look half-eaten. Maggie usually let it go figuring that at least her daughter would be getting the *essence* of a vegetable in her body ...

"Of course," Maggie said. "You know the drill, though: Clean up after yourselves."

Eva took off, her footfalls distinct across squeaky old floorboards, the sound bringing back memories in torrents. Maggie scooped up a few rags and dropped them into a bucket. As she listened to Eva banter like a mini-me and Siena giggle in response, she remembered the days of eating breakfast before the beach, lunch after the beach, and being called in for dinner at twilight by the commanding voice of their father ... after their mother's less convincing voice had been ignored.

Oh, there were other memories, ones far less soothing. Like the times work dried up for their dad and they'd have to pack up and move off to wherever the next meal came from. Eventually, they all settled outside of Phoenix, which is where Maggie also put down roots. Her siblings, though, ran off to where school and work took them. And soon after, her parents decided to do missionary work for a few years. When Maggie's husband left, and with her family flung farther than a quick drive away, those carefree days of running around the old beach house seemed more like an old black-and-white movie than real life.

And then there was that last summer here, the one where she had come full of hope for a future that turned a one-eighty faster than an aerial on a hollow wave. Maggie peeked down the hall. The girls were quiet now, so she padded along the floorboards until catching sight of them beneath that ancient map that hung proudly over the dining room's forever-scarred table. So far, neither Grace nor Jake nor Maggie could remove that map—or the table. Too many memories attached to them both.

Luke hadn't yet given her details about what happened with CeCe, so she could only guess. Maybe he would even tell her everything tonight—though she still could hardly believe she had agreed to spending time alone with him. This complicated things more than ever. She'd long known that divorce was a last resort, something that God allowed, but only in specific circumstances.

Abandonment was one of those circumstances—and something she had experienced herself.

Maggie closed her eyes, thinking. She had never been a fan of CeCe, but desert her child? Even Maggie could not attach something so unthinkable to her past nemesis. Was CeCe around here still? Did Siena ever see her mother? Maggie puttered around the living room, stacking magazines and brushing crumbs off of the coffee table and into her hands. By the sound of their chatter about the beach and the fun things they had been learning, neither girl seemed to be harboring feelings of abandonment. Maggie had worked hard to instill confidence and love in Eva, and by the looks of things, Luke had done the same with Siena.

Luke.

She closed her eyes, trying to shut out the sight of him, all sculpted six feet of him. That swath of stubble over his mouth, lips pursed as he considered her, penetrating eyes that watched her, almost thoughtfully. Even that scar intrigued her. Everything about him was familiar and yet new, too. He'd aged, as had she, but he'd done it well. So, so well. His bronze and skinny teenaged layers, earned from years of growing up on the beach and in the water, had filled out now into a more chiseled form.

Exactly when did she start thinking of the guy who slit her heart in two as more than just that?

Honestly, Maggie had half-expected to find Luke with a beer gut and untoned arms. If she were honest, she had practically wished that on him, part of her mental skewering of an old boyfriend who had done her wrong. She huffed a laugh.

"Mom?"

Maggie jerked a look up. Both girls were watching her from the table, with Eva wearing a particularly concerned expression.

"You look weird. What were you laughing at?"

Siena's round eyes watched her, too, a curious glint in her smile. "You look like my dad when he's counting his steps."

"Counting his steps?"

"Yeah, he's *obsessed* with some app on his phone."

"Oh, well"—Maggie glanced at Siena—"I was just thinking of something funny. Like that joke you told me today."

Siena smiled but Eva rolled her eyes. "That was *hours* ago, Mom."

Maggie grabbed an empty bowl from the coffee table and headed to the kitchen. "Well, then, don't mind me," she sang out. Out of the girls' sight, she dumped the bowl into the sink and leaned against the edge, trying to get her bearings. She gave her head a slight shake, a warning filling her head. Yes, Luke's news that he and CeCe were no longer a happy couple complicated everything.

She huffed a sigh rather aggressively and spun back

toward the sink. *Whatever you do, Maggie, don't get too attached.*

"HAND ME THAT BLOCK PLANER, will you?" Luke looked through his goggles to his new intern, Carlos. He'd met the kid on the beach after the teen had crushed a bomb of a wave. They'd struck up a conversation and Luke offered him a summer job learning the art of board shaping. He learned later that Carlos's Uncle Miguel was the pastor of the church he sometimes attended.

Behind a mask of his own, Carlos plucked the block off a shelf and planted it in Luke's gloved hand. He stood back and lifted his mask. "Not gonna use a template?"

Luke shook his head. "Going old-school on this one." Board shapers often lay a template over a blank of foam to know where to cut.

Carlos laughed. "Aw, man, my mom would say you're like Michelangelo. Only instead of stone, you're lookin' at a blank with a surfboard in it somewhere."

Luke grinned.

"My mom's an art teacher," Carlos added. "Tells me all kinds of stuff like that."

"Keep listening to your mom."

Carlos laughed. "Okay if I go on my break now?"

Luke nodded and dipped his chin down again, intending to focus on the task in front of him. The kid was right, in a way. The blank of foam, if viewed by a creative and focused mind, would become what it was meant to be.

He reached his hands over the board and stopped, a

niggling of something uncomfortable rising inside him. *Keep listening to your mom.* He could never deliver those same words to Siena and that fact haunted him. Even today. To strangers in that ice cream shop, everything about today looked so normal. Happy, tired kids getting ice cream with two patient adults on hand to pay the bill and laugh at the banter.

An ache that had formed in his chest earlier while inside that ice cream parlor began to bellow now. He replayed the moment Maggie finally allowed her eyes to catch with his. They were brown and held flecks of jade and sunlight. She had shown up in cottony sweats that clung to her curves and he'd had to wipe away the sweat from his forehead more than once.

Hopefully, if she noticed, she hadn't been grossed out by him.

Luke glanced down at the shapeless board as it waited for him, knowing it would stay in its current state for another day. Even Michelangelo would find it difficult to find focus through the mess of thoughts that had outdone him today. Maggie had awakened something in him that he figured was dead. He had always considered her cute. Real cute. But the woman who strolled into his heart today had sashayed right past cuteness. He had the suspicion that, given the chance, she could take him down, mind, body, and soul, with a flick of her hair and one well-placed *yes.*

Luke's heart rate accelerated.

Steady, boy. Another ache, one sharper and more pronounced, poked at him. The one that reminded him that she—and Eva—would be leaving soon. He couldn't let himself get too attached. Not again. Wouldn't be good for

Siena, nor him. So why had he asked her out tonight? Was that wise?

Luke rubbed a palm across the back of his neck. He didn't care to relive the last night he and Maggie had seen each other more than ten years ago, the memory surprisingly clear. Admittedly, he was a jerk that night, but in his defense, it had been his way of dealing with his own troubles.

If only she knew it had nothing to do with her.

Of course, it didn't take her long to run off with Rafael. He curled his hands into fists, thinking of seeing them together the very next morning when he wandered out to the beach, not that it was any of his business. Luke removed his gloves. He laid his goggles on the workbench and turned around, leaning against it. He crossed his arms and dropped his chin to his chest, the pull and stretch to his neck bringing relief.

Siena's cherub-like face sprang to his mind, erasing his wayward thoughts, and he smiled. His daughter had been his break in the storm, the very reason not to let regrets have their place. Ruefully, he realized that he needed to be careful, not only for his own sake but for Siena's as well. His daughter had been hurt enough.

Whatever you do, dude, don't get too attached. Luke sighed and picked up his phone. He punched in Pastor Miguel's number and waited.

THE AIR WAS STILL, yet brisk. Maggie zipped her puffy jacket to her chin and tucked her hands into her pockets.

"Are you too cold to walk to the restaurant?" Luke asked. "We can take my car."

"No, not at all. I love walking."

"You always did."

"I still do." She sighed. "Besides, you'll get all your steps in this way."

Luke sucked in a breath. "What?"

Maggie wrinkled her nose, smiling. "Siena told me about your obsession with some fitness app on your phone."

"Did she now?" He laughed freely at that.

Maggie laughed lightly and together they walked along the familiar path to downtown, talking only sparingly, as if not needing to fill the quiet night with chatter. Much of what they passed hadn't changed. Some of the houses—bungalows, really—had been cleared to make way for larger, more modern homes made of sustainable materials.

But most had stayed the same as they had always been, their yards neat and porches wide, stuck in time. Her eyes trailed along the fence that surrounded the old church they sometimes attended. It looked abandoned except for the scaffolding on one side. New paint job? Maggie made a mental note to see if services were still being held there.

They reached Giovanni's. Though new to her, the restaurant's brick and vine-covered entry gave it an Old World feel.

Luke held the door. "After you, Mags."

Like the walk over here, much about Luke felt the same as before, too. The way he hopped on and off curbs periodically as they made small talk, the funny pitch of his laugh whenever he found something particularly hilarious. But in some ways, like when he held the door and watched her walk inside the restaurant ahead of him, a smile warming his face, she felt as if she were getting a new and grown-up version of the surfer kid she once knew.

It stirred something fresh and intriguing within her.

Inside, the host picked up two menus. "Right this way."

They sat across from each other, the place a caricature of every Italian movie she'd ever seen. Red-and-white checkered tablecloth, a fiasco—a fat Chianti bottle—overflowing with wax from a taper candle, and accordion music playing in the background. Her mother would have loved this place.

"What sounds good to you?" he asked.

She glanced up at him, the flicker of candlelight dancing across his handsome face, but she dared not answer his question truthfully. Instead, she shut her menu. "Why don't you order for us?"

"Sure about that? I might order the snails."

"This isn't a French place."

"Italy has snails too."

"In their gardens, maybe."

He laughed and shut his menu. When their waiter brought glasses of water, Luke handed him both menus. "We'll have a pizza formaggi, spaghetti with meatballs, a couple of Caesar salads, and a bottle of your house red."

"Wow," Maggie said when the waiter had gone, "are we expecting anyone else to join us?"

He hunched forward and gazed at her through thick lashes. "I'd chase them away if they showed up."

Quietly, a server brought over a bottle of wine and two glasses and filled them both before padding away.

Luke lifted a glass. "Cheers."

She sipped her wine, fruit forward but drier on the finish, and determined not to let it go to her head. But he had ordered a bottle, and by the looks of it, they still had a long way to go. Good thing they had walked.

Their salads arrived. Luke took a bite, savoring it. He looked earnestly into Maggie's eyes, as if readying himself, and said, "CeCe has a drug addiction and she has for most of our marriage."

"Oh. That's ... terrible."

He shrugged. "I rarely talk about it anymore. You know that stuff—pot, pills, cigs—it was all over the place when we were teens."

"No, I really didn't know that." She shrugged. "Was never interested."

He nodded, assessing her, his mouth grim. "Yeah, I remember that you didn't care about any of that stuff. Your mom and dad obviously instilled a healthy fear of drugs in you and your siblings."

"Actually, they instilled a healthy fear of *them* in us."

Luke grinned. "Knowing your father, I have no doubt. I assure you, though, that buying your drug of choice on the beach in summer was as easy as digging up a sand crab."

She took another sip of wine, as did he. They sat in silence a moment, Luke watching her, as if waiting for some kind of reaction.

"So what now, Luke?" she finally asked. "I know you say your marriage is done, but I can't believe CeCe would turn in her Mom card."

"Truth is, Mags, she's not interested in being a mother or being married to me. It's one sad chapter that'll never go away because ..."

He sat back and looked into the distance, as if his appetite had gone.

"Because you have Siena."

Luke swung a gaze back to Maggie. "Exactly. If not for Siena being in my life, I wouldn't know half of what I've learned about addiction and its effect on a family." He held that gaze on her. "Of course ..."

"You don't have to say it."

"I know that, but it's what you're thinking."

Maggie gave him a pointed look. "You don't know what I'm thinking."

Luke raised his brows at her, as if to say *Oh, really?*

Maggie continued to stare at him, refusing to cave.

He leaned forward again, sadness drawing on his features. "You win. I'll confess: If CeCe and I, well, if I hadn't gotten her pregnant, none of this mess would have happened, and maybe you and—"

"Stop." Maggie put down her glass of wine, shaking her head. "I don't want to think about those days, Luke."

"This coming from the girl who never liked to put an issue to rest until she had turned it inside out and examined every angle."

"What does that mean?"

"You don't remember how you used to ask a million questions about surfing? How do you know what size board to get? How hard is it to stand up? Where's the best place to surf?" He gave her a half-smile. "You were the one who talked me into all of that, you know."

She knew. He'd had a fear of the water when they were young. Maggie had almost forgotten about that. But one day, after watching him mentally trying to talk himself into getting into the ocean, she encouraged him to face his fear. If only she'd stopped there. It pained her to think about how often she had pushed him to give competing a try.

He continued. "You never got the credit you deserved."

"Not that I mattered much once you started winning ..."

Luke reacted like she'd sucker punched him. He sat back and folded his arms. "You held your own."

"Whatever that means."

"C'mon, Mags." His smile was careful, broaching. "I know I was a jerk, but it didn't take long for you to fill my shoes with some ... lowlife."

Maggie set her jaw. Really? Hadn't he just said that maybe she and he could've had a shot? But now he's blaming it on her? She narrowed her eyes. She wouldn't stand for him blaming her for marrying soon after he announced that he would be marrying CeCe—who was pregnant with his child, by the way.

Luke sighed. "Sorry. Didn't mean that."

Maggie bit her lip, her eyes still small as slits. Part of her wanted to stand up and walk out the door and never talk to him again. Maybe she'd slam the door on her way out, like some drama queen. She'd managed to stay away before—and she could do it again!

But the other part ... she breathed in and out slowly. The other part of her wanted to stand her ground and fight. Despite the deep guilt she carried with her, they'd both made mistakes that had led them here. "You invited me to dinner so you could blame me for what *you* did a decade ago? I won't let you turn the tables on this."

Luke's eyes widened, as if stricken. "Wait." He reached out and grasped Maggie's hand, no doubt feeling it stiffen in his grip. "I did not mean to bring up any of that. I'm sorry. I-I got caught up in the past." He huffed a sigh. "Forgive me."

She stuck her tongue in her cheek and flicked a look at him. A tug-of-war had been going on inside her heart all day, and she didn't know what to make of it. It's not as if they could go back and change anything that had happened. If only they could bury all the bad memories, once and for all.

Maggie slowly pulled her hand away from Luke's. She flashed him a look. "Let's be honest—neither of us is unhappy about the way things turned out."

Luke was silent a moment. "Well, I wouldn't exactly say that."

She paused, suddenly having a very difficult time making eye contact with him. But she forced herself. "You have Siena. And I have Eva. Is that a better way of putting it?"

He lowered his gaze to his wine glass before looking up again. "When you say it like that, you're right. I wouldn't put it any other way either."

Their server appeared with a steaming pizza and set it on a wire rack between them. Another server brought two plates of spaghetti and meatballs. The tense moment lessened with the arrival of food, but more than that had occurred, Maggie thought. Time had blurred the details of their past. She determined to focus on the here—and the now—while also pushing away warning bells of regret and second-guessing.

Maggie turned her attention to the vast amounts of food, unsure if she would be able to consume a noticeable portion of any of it. Still, the timing was perfect. The arrival of dinner had helped derail any more discussion about the night she and Luke had split up for good. Truthfully, she didn't care to think—or talk—about that time in their lives ever again.

Luke gestured to the pizza. "Dig in."

She bit into a slice of pizza and closed her eyes.

"That good, eh?"

Maggie opened her eyes to find Luke staring back at her, a teasing smile on his face. "It's amazing."

"Wait'll you try the meatballs. Really glad you aren't a vegetarian anymore."

"Me too." She twirled her fork in the spaghetti. "Despite all that's happened with CeCe, Siena is a really great kid, Luke." Maggie continued to twirl her fork, thinking. She didn't add that the bond Eva and Siena shared had begun to stir up additional stress and worry in her plans. Perhaps she could find a way to keep their friendship alive. And then when they were older—

"I think so, too," he said, interrupting her musings. "Fortunately, Siena doesn't remember the terrible times much at all. Most of it happened when she was a baby. I've done my best to shield her from issues that crop up sometimes, to give her a happy home, despite the hole her mother's absence has created."

The hole her mother's absence has created ...

Inwardly, Maggie berated herself. She hadn't considered that Luke might have changed, that he was no longer the selfish up-and-coming surf champ who had taken advantage of her only to run off with someone else. She realized, with chest-tightening clarity, that he had grown up, just as she had. And that the secret she held so close to her heart was actually a much larger problem than she realized.

Truly, the last person she had wanted to run into when

she got to Colibri was Luke. So much time had lapsed since the night they had ended it, or rather, he had ended it. After that night, they saw each other once, only briefly, and then? It was as if their longtime, often long-distance, love affair had never even existed.

For a while, that's what hurt the most.

But she'd had to let it go.

She put down her fork. After taking a sip of wine, she watched Luke over the rim of her glass. "I'm glad we both came through those years unscathed." She said this despite the secret, and the truth that she had no job or home to go back to when her time in Colibri was up. But, still.

"But?" he asked.

"But nothing."

Luke's forehead flickered with doubt. "You were right when you said that neither of us is unhappy about our outcomes. My daughter is ..." He smiled. "Well, she's taught me how to love. I'd do anything for her."

"That's beautiful. I feel the same way about Eva."

"But it's not true, at least for me, that I've come through the years unscathed."

"Hmm."

Luke rubbed the back of his neck in that old, familiar way, eyeing her. "I've missed you, Mags."

"We were kids, Luke."

"We were young adults."

"Technically, maybe. But young adults without a shred of maturity."

He gave her a rueful look. "Well, that changed in a hurry, didn't it?"

She returned his rueful gaze.

"So," he said, "about us."

"Us?"

The corners of his eyes dipped. "Yeah. I miss what we had."

What was he saying? That he wanted to return to the way things were before the breakup? To when they were kids hoping for a future yet ill-equipped to make that happen? He couldn't possibly mean that, not with his marriage in tatters. Nor could she agree to pursing something that had died its rightful death. Not now. Especially not with so much of her life in tangles.

"You mean our friendship," she said.

He seemed to weigh that. "Yes."

Her heightened sense of anxiety lowered considerably. He wanted to be friends. She couldn't fathom that, really. Not in the traditional way. But, for now, while she was still in Colibri for a short while longer, it wouldn't hurt to be friends.

"I'm here with you now, Luke, so I suppose it's possible that we could be ... friends again."

Luke lifted his glass, his eyes imploring her. "Anything is possible."

She smiled.

"Let's drink to that," Luke said.

She clinked her glass against his. "Cheers."

6

Friends. It was a start.

Luke pulled off his goggles and his gloves and placed them on the scarred-up old counter in his workroom. He stood back and admired his progress on the blank, Carlos's comments not far from his mind. The emerging board might not be a masterpiece, but the more he refined its shape and smoothed its edges, he could see it taking on a life.

Kind of like his thoughts. Last night had been a mixed bag of emotions, and he had nearly upended the dinner before it began. But he wouldn't change it. They had tussled some, and somewhere between holding the door for Maggie as she stepped inside and their first sip of wine, he knew what he had hoped to gain, and that was to reignite what had been snuffed out between them.

First thing this morning, on his pastor's advice, he made another step toward that end.

A commotion in the shop caught his attention. He

grabbed a towel and wiped his hands with it as he walked out to the front.

"Hey, Stringbean!"

"Hey, yourself, Pincher." Luke laughed at the sight of the burly guy with a buzz cut and a signature scar above his left brow.

Carlos, who was manning the shop for the day, raised his brows. "*The* Pincher?"

Luke nodded. "Yup. Hey, Pinch, I'd like you to meet my right-hand guy here, Carlos."

"Hey, man, you're a legend," Carlos said, pumping the guy's hand.

"Great to meet you, though I don't know why you'd work for this guy over here."

Carlos chuckled. "He's not so bad."

Luke shot his intern a mock scowl.

"I mean," Carlos cut in, "he's a great boss. Totally forgot they called him *Stringbean*, though."

Luke's gut sank a little but he kept a smile on his face. He'd mostly forgotten about that too. He shook off thoughts of the past and instead eyed the infamous semi-pro surfer from their teen years who had entered his shop. "What's brought you by?"

"Gotta proposition for ya."

"Shoot."

Pincher walked over to the window and pointed at a flyer. "One of the sponsors of Ringer fell out. Gonna need someone like yourself to fatten up the pot again. You in?"

"Whoa. Seriously? You're just going to come in here after how many years and ask me for money?"

Pincher raised a brow. "Ya want me to take you to dinner first?"

Carlos cackled. "That's good, bro."

Pincher craned his neck left and right, looking around the shop. "It'll be good advertising for this dive."

Yeah, it would. Luke had long been out of competing, but he'd seen the kind of plug sponsors could get, especially if the waves cooperated. Being with Maggie last night brought some of those memories back.

Chalk up another reason to pursue the charming Maggie Holloway. He sighed in mock exasperation. "Why not? Yeah, I'll help out."

Pincher smiled widely. "Excellent." He plopped a card into Luke's hand. "Email over your logo and any other graphics you want us to highlight. I'll have my money people call your money people—"

"AKA me."

"Tryin' to be all profesh here, dude, but okay. I'll have the group's treasurer call you. Got it?"

"Got it."

Pincher stepped toward the door and stopped. A phone rang in the background. "Hey, Stringbean?"

"Yup?"

"Thanks, man. Really appreciate it."

As Pincher left, Carlos appeared at Luke's side. "Phone's for you."

"Thanks." Luke took it from him. "Hello?"

"Luke, it's me."

His veins filled with blood that had turned cold at the sound of his estranged wife's voice. "Hi."

"Got your message, and why not. I'm ready to sign the papers."

He nodded, a slight rise in his body temperature. "Good news. I'll send—"

"Wait. On one condition."

Luke shut his eyes. He was tired of this and had hoped, for only a second or two, that there would be no more games. So much for miracles.

She continued, "I want you to come pick them up."

Luke waited. He assumed she would ask to see Siena, perhaps even make a relationship with her a condition of signing the papers. Staying in contact with CeCe had become unbearable to him, and yet, in the long run, he knew doing so would be the best for their daughter.

He was about to tell CeCe that he could come tomorrow, and that he would bring Siena with him, when she said, "Alone."

Luke sucked in a breath.

"I'll sign the divorce papers and you can pick them up," CeCe said. "But I want you to come alone."

He hung up, his first thought to pick up the project he'd been working on and pitch it against the wall. But Pastor Miguel's words from their phone conversation stopped him. *You have to forgive yourself, Luke, to move on, but you must also forgive CeCe. You won't rest until you do.*

With the shop momentarily quiet, Luke stopped, closed his eyes, and asked God how he could possibly do that.

MAGGIE HAD THOUGHT about Luke all night long. The way he walked in near silence next to her, yet made her feel anything but alone. How his hand brushed hers more than once. The heat of his gaze whenever he turned to her as they walked along. When they reached the restaurant and he opened the door for her, she stole a glance at his full height, his face freshly shorn, the sun's afterglow in his eyes.

How in the world would she get anything done today? She was already having a difficult time holding to the concept of "friendship."

Still, another week was in the books and she still had a heap of touching up to do. Plus, she had promised to cut and style Brooke Lamont's hair—the owner of the new bakery in town, sometime this weekend. How would she explain these loose ends to her siblings during their weekly call tomorrow? She shook off the picture in her head of Lacy, who would probably throw some shade her way—and hold a glass of wine while doing it.

Maggie put a hand on her hip, and blew out a breath. Time was ticking, more than she wanted to admit. *Focus, focus.*

She surveyed the hall, her plans dashed. She had been hoping that cleaning the walls with a sponge eraser would be enough, but nuh-uh. The long hallway was still dingy and pale. With resolve, she retrieved a tarp from the garage, dragged it back inside, unrolled it, and began taping down the edges.

While Maggie was on her haunches, Eva slid down the hall in her socks, crinkling the tarp as she tumbled along. "What in the world?"

Eva let loose her high-pitched laugh, the one that had the power to shake the roof.

Maggie playfully swatted at her daughter's ankles. "Get off of here right now!"

As if she had suddenly lost her hearing, Eva plopped onto the tarp that lay across the floor. She looked up at her mom. "So can Siena come over? Her dad has to go somewhere all day and she doesn't want to stay at her grandma's. She says it's super boring over there."

Maggie sat back on her heels and her gaze darted to the clock over in the kitchen. Had Luke called her? Her phone was still upstairs, plugged into a charger. And what would she have said if he had asked for this favor? After last night, the weight of her secret had shifted and she no longer felt as if she had the upper hand.

On the contrary, at the moment, Maggie felt very, very small.

She returned her gaze to Eva, moving back into mom mode. "You sure? I'm pretty much stuck here all day painting and won't be able to take you anywhere."

Eva scrambled to her feet. "Yeah. We're fine."

"Okay, then. If her dad can drop her off, I'm okay with it."

"Cool!"

As Eva took off down the hall, Maggie began to plot out her next few hours while using a rag to dry off some of her attempts at erasing years of dirt. Still, Luke would be here soon. Maybe she should run upstairs and put some makeup on, just in case he came inside when he dropped off Siena. *So much for her inner warning not to get too attached.*

How dense was she? She would be gone from Colibri in less than two weeks. Besides, there was no doubt in her mind that what she currently felt for Luke was a resurrected childhood crush—one that had ended very badly the first time.

What they had last night felt ... good. A friendship reborn. Why mess that up with thoughts of anything more? Maybe CeCe would get better and they would rekindle what they once had? For Siena's sake, she hoped that could come to pass.

Maggie inhaled and shut her eyes. Did she really want to see a repeat of the heartache she had once endured?

She pitched a rag onto the ground. If Luke didn't like what he saw, why did she care? Besides, she was doing that man a *favor* by babysitting his, well, his pre-teen. He'd have to live with seeing her in her current state. Case closed.

Maggie twisted her hair into a knot and clipped it to the top of her head. She began the tedious job of cutting in the paint around the edges of the walls and ceiling. By the time the bell rang and Eva skidded into the living room to answer the door, Maggie was elbows deep into her project. Luke would probably drop off Siena and leave right away anyway.

"Wow. You've done some serious work on this place." Luke's voice floated smoothly into the room. He had an appraising smile on his face and she wanted to die. To pound out a hole in the wall, slither inside, and pull the busted drywall in with her. Why again had she decided not to at least dab on some powder or gloss her lips?

Abruptly, she stood, her hand cramping from her tight grip on a paintbrush handle. "Hey," she said.

"Hey, yourself." Luke's dark brown hair curved away from his face, like it had been blown by the wind, his skin golden. Last night he had worn dark jeans, a black T-shirt, and a smoke-colored blazer. Today he was in blue jeans and a T-shirt that hugged his body and held on for dear life.

Not that she noticed all that.

She turned away, keeping her eyes focused on the partially painted wall in front of her. Maybe if she couldn't see him, he could not see her. Worked for cats.

He cleared his voice. "So, thanks for keeping Siena today." He paused. "Sure you don't mind?"

Of course she didn't mind. She wasn't some ... ogre. Maggie swallowed a sigh and turned her chin enough to let him know she could hear him. "Not at all. Siena's a sweetheart. I did tell Eva, though, that I wouldn't be able to take them anywhere today. Hopefully they won't get too bored hanging around the house."

He smiled back at her. "I can't imagine that."

She wanted to ask where he was going, but was it any of her business? Sadly, no. Unless he was just planning to shape boards in the shop today and wanted to do so without any interruptions, but wouldn't he say so? Maybe he had a girlfriend somewhere and was taking her wine tasting or something. Gah. Now she was babysitting so Luke could go on a date. Perfect.

"Maggie?"

Luke's voice, thick and low, startled her out of her thoughts. "Hmm?"

"I really appreciate this."

She put down the paintbrush and looked him in the eye. He looked back. That same sadness she had noticed in recent days shone in his gaze like a dimly lit vessel. She had no idea what to make of it but inexplicably wanted desperately to make it go away. Heat crept into her face at the intimate thought.

"It's no trouble, Luke," she whispered. "Truly."

After he had gone, Maggie continued to think about Luke. Though he looked and smelled amazing, and she feared he was off to meet up with one of his many admirers, she could not shake off the sense that something was off with him today.

The girls showed up at the end of the hall and pulled her out of her musings. Eva held her boogie board in front of her. "Mom, can we—"

"No."

"You don't even know what I was going to ask."

Maggie raised a brow toward her daughter. "Oh, really? You're holding a boogie board."

Eva smiled guiltily. "So ...?"

Maggie wagged her head, looking pointedly at each girl. "I need you both to promise me that if you go outside, you'll stay together and always stay in view of the house. Okay?"

Eva pouted, but Siena piped up, "Oh, we will, Maggie. We promise."

"Good," Maggie said, glancing at Eva. "Now put the boogie board back. Maybe we can figure out a time to use it after camp one day next week."

Eva began to roll her eyes, but Maggie stopped her with a quick "look."

"Fine," Eva said, and headed back to her bedroom with the boogie board, Siena following closely behind her.

Satisfied that she had made herself clear, Maggie returned to her DIY painting project, determined to roll out the entire hall as quickly as possible. Soon enough she would need to hand over the keys to Lacy and she had yet to determine where she and Eva would go when the time came. With Eva's pre-teen attitude showing signs of rebellion, Maggie wanted to replant their roots as soon as possible.

The thought should have lifted Maggie's spirits but instead brought a slight ache to her heart. Arizona suddenly felt like a long way from Colibri Beach.

"Did you really turn the guest bath into a salon?"

Maggie scoffed. Sunday night had come and Lacy peered at Maggie through the screen, a smirk of a smile on her face. The rest of the clan looked impatient as they waited for a virtual update about the house, but all Maggie could think about was how she was suddenly not ready for her time in Colibri Beach to end.

"Don't be ridiculous," Maggie retorted. "Just trying to be resourceful while I'm here."

She was getting tired of Lacy's needling comments, some of them quite cryptic. Week after week Lacy had managed to drop in some kind of dig at one or all of her siblings. Well. Her turn at the beach house was coming soon, and she would find out firsthand how it felt to relive one's childhood while dodging no-so-favorite memories, all while doing the grunt work that came with the inheritance.

Grace cut in, her voice kind, but probing. "How is the hunt for a new salon coming? Have you found a spot? And an apartment too?"

"Working on it," she said, deflecting.

"How so?" Lacy inquired.

Maggie touched her forehead with her hand and rubbed a spot of sharp pain. "How so what?"

"How are you working on it? Because all I've seen so far is you splashing a little paint on the wall and hanging out at the beach." Lacy looked pointedly into the webcam. "By the way, see anything you like?"

Maggie frowned.

Bella piped up. "I think Maggie's doing a great job. Be nice, Lacy."

Lacy shook her head and muttered something difficult to hear.

"What's up, Lacy?" Grace asked. "If there's something bothering you, you should say what it is. Be specific."

Leave it to a lawyer to press for the facts.

One of Lacy's eyebrows shot up. "Fine. I'll say what we all know: Maggie broke our parents' hearts."

The call erupted into a spattering of gasps and protests.

Jake said, "I don't recall anything like that. And frankly—"

"And frankly what?" Lacy said. "You don't have time for the drama? Too many *important* meetings to attend to protect all your billions?"

"Stop it," Grace said. "You're being dumb. You know that?"

"Dumb? Is that what you say to witnesses when they're on the stand? Or your clients when you don't agree with them?"

Maggie quietly got up, stepped down the hall to Eva's door, and shut it before returning to the call. Her siblings continued to squabble as if Maggie wasn't hearing all of it. She sat down, took a deep breath before speaking. "I think that, whatever this is, it's between Lacy and me. I will say, to all of you, that I made some mistakes when I was young. We all know it. But"—her voice caught and she momentarily put a hand to her mouth—"despite my ill-fated marriage, Mom and Dad absolutely doted on Eva. Your niece's life is the ... well, it's the very example of grace. I didn't deserve that kid, but she's mine anyway. I'm forever grateful for that favor in my life."

The room fell quiet.

"Now," Maggie continued, "let me catch you up on where I am with painting and what Lacy will have to deal with when she takes over in a couple of weeks."

7

L uke sat on his back porch, the signed papers in his hands. He wagged his head. How many years ago had these divorce papers been drawn up? Didn't matter now. He had called his attorney, who assured him they were still valid, that all he needed was CeCe's signature —and he would be a free man. Finally.

He glanced out at the marshy dunes, an odd mixture of elation and sadness blowing through his heart and mind. What had become of CeCe was nothing short of tragic. The fact that he could now legally be free of a woman who had long ago abandoned him, and Siena, did not change the hard truth that his ex-wife was, once again, in rehab. And that she had no thought of ever bonding with the daughter she had left behind. Guilt gnawed at Luke and he began to wonder if the churning in his gut would ever ebb away. Would he always wonder how much his actions had played into CeCe's decisions?

Luke's mind wandered back to when Siena was still a

baby. CeCe had disappeared one evening and when she stumbled in, her eyes unfocused slits, Luke was in denial. She had promised not to get high anymore. He could not believe that she would break her word, not with a child who looked to her for daily care ... and love.

"You promised," he said.

CeCe laughed, the effect sharp and caustic. She stuck a pointy finger in his face. "You're the one who turned back on all your *promises!*"

He shifted, looking directly at her. "Which ones, CeCe? The one where I promised to marry you? To raise our child together? To support you so you could follow your dream of becoming a chef?"

Her nose flared. "You were a big deal when I married you —a real big shot. Now you're just a, a *has-been!*"

Maybe she had been right. When they met, he had been competing in the surf circuit, had won a heap of prize money, and had earned the confidence of sponsors. He had also attracted the attention of scores of girls who had not been coy about what they were after when it came to him. For a time, he loved every minute of the attention, not to mention the financial benefits and sponsor gifts.

But then everything changed. He couldn't do it anymore —he wouldn't.

But why did that matter? He invested his winnings well. Earned a good living. Doted on Siena. Why wasn't that enough?

He stopped asking himself those questions years ago. The answers no longer mattered. He had hoped to make a clean break of things, to raise Siena in a happy home, and to pursue good, honest work. And he had nearly given up asking CeCe, again, to sign the papers necessary to make that final break a reality.

Until Maggie showed up in Colibri.

Maggie had already told him she didn't care to think of the past, but he could never forget it. Luke sucked in a breath. He ran a hand across the side of his head, his fingers tangling with his hair. Breaking up with Maggie was the hardest thing he had ever done. Much more difficult than separating from CeCe, if he were honest.

And that was because ... he loved her. Luke had always loved Maggie.

If only ... if only he hadn't bought the lie, the lie that told him he was some *big shot*. He shook his head. The girls were everywhere back then. Groupies showed up at his house. They'd follow him to the beach and camp out. And they would photobomb him whenever he won—long before photobombing was a thing.

Of all the girls who followed him around in those days, CeCe was the most persistent. Legs for days, she followed him around until he took a second look. And then he'd done much more than look. Luke regretted the night he had spent with CeCe, his only hope that it meant as little to her as it did to him.

Maggie's family showed up in Colibri less than two weeks later. She was no longer the teenager who had left the beach the year before, the one he'd kept up with all year with phone calls and emails. He had even sent her a "Wish You Were Here" postcard. She'd sent one back, stained with lipstick, her lips pressed into a kiss. By the time she landed back on the coast, she had already finished a year at beauty school and was flush with excitement that she had passed her licensing examinations.

Luke would never forget seeing her for the first time that summer. She was ... hot. Eye-popping, heat-making, no-longer-a-girl sexy. He had wanted to throw a blanket over her bikini-wearing self and protect her from, well, guys like him.

On that day that he remembered so well, Maggie ran up to him in her yellow bikini, threw her tan arms around his neck, and kissed him playfully on the mouth. She pulled back from him, laughter fluttering out of her like a million bells, sending his twenty-year-old self into a tailspin from which he could not emerge.

"I've missed you," she said, her breath like sweet wine, her skin reminding him of coconut oil and wildflowers.

"Not as much as I've missed you," he'd told her after he had been able to catch his breath.

And that night, when the wind had blown away the clouds and left behind a dark blanket poked full of stars, they'd made love out on the beach, in a cradle between the dunes.

Luke's heart pounded in his ears and he awoke from the memories that he once thought were scattered on the breeze forever. Another thought darkened his mind, harsh words spoken by CeCe, long after he had married her and Maggie had moved away.

"Even after you got me, you wanted that maggot," CeCe had spat at him one night. Then she laughed that horrible, air-piercing laugh, the one that always indicated when her spiral had begun. "I did that girl a favor, Luke. She ran off and found *her* true love. Bet *he* didn't let her down. Maggie Holloway owes me!"

Luke's heart slowed to a painful thud, CeCe's rejection of him brutal and mind numbing

But in the end, he realized that CeCe was right. Despite the fame, the girls, the money ... CeCe's pregnancy, he wanted Maggie. Always had.

His breath caught in his lungs. It was now or never, but what ... what would happen if he told her how he felt? That he loved her now and always would? Would she trust him and stay? Or spin around and leave him here with his heart in his hands?

His mind spiraled back. That night ... that terrible night, when he had told her about the baby, Maggie had not missed a beat. She flew right into the arms of ... Rafael.

The idea of it made him gag. Even today, he could barely look at the guy, and he assumed the feeling was mutual: Rafael had not once set foot in his shop.

Not long after that night, the news hit him with a one-two punch. Not that he didn't deserve it. Maggie had married. He assumed she had found a way to rope in Colibri's resident shirtless bad boy, but then he'd seen Rafael around the beach. Eventually, Luke learned the truth: Maggie had eloped with a guy from her hometown in Arizona who had been chasing after her for years.

She'd finally been caught.

Luke reflected back. Maggie had been able to shrug off their break-up fast enough to turn around and marry another guy. Could he stand it if he professed his love for her again, after all this time apart, and she left Colibri anyway?

"You can't leave!" Brooke Lamont, owner of Brooke's Beachside Bakery, turned her chin from side to side, admiring the cut and style Maggie had done for her. Lea had sung Maggie's praises, so the baker had insisted on making an appointment before the month was up. "We need you, Maggie. Sure you won't change your mind and stay?"

A loaded question if she had ever heard one. Maggie sighed. The thought of staying in Colibri Beach had come to her more than once, but so did a barrage of open-ended questions.

Could she drum up enough business here?

Where would they live once the beach house was sold?

The biggest question hanging over her was the truth that she had been keeping from Luke. At her mother's and Greg's urging, she had promised never to tell anyone that Luke was Eva's father. Maggie had kept her promise, always believing it was for the best. Luke was married with his own child on the way, and his new wife hated her—she'd been on the receiving end of CeCe's knife-wielding gaze often enough to know that. But now, the two people who knew the truth were gone—one by choice. What now?

If she told Luke, he would never forgive her and the lie would unravel their truce. Wasn't it better to keep it close to her heart, especially with all the turmoil going on in Luke's life right now? Not to mention her own. Maggie's heart squeezed at the prospect of what telling him the truth would look like.

Clearly, Brooke had made an impossible suggestion.

Maggie fiddled with the front tendrils of Brooke's hair. "You're too kind. Thank you for the vote of confidence."

"So you're saying I haven't convinced you."

Maggie shrugged and smiled. "I'd love to, but I also want to provide routine for Eva, and I think wrapping things up and going home would be the best way to do that. Know what I mean?"

Brooke sighed. "I think so. I'm not a mom yet, but you're probably thinking about back-to-school shopping, a regular bedtime, reacquainting her with friends. Things like that, right?"

Maggie broke out in a smile. "Wow, you're good. You'll make a great momma someday." She paused. "Is that your boyfriend I've seen at the bakery?"

"Trent? Yes, we're—well, yes. He's my boyfriend."

"I take it this is something new?"

It was Brooke's turn to shrug. "Not exactly new, but I'm also not sure where we're headed, you know? Though, well, I *hope* it's somewhere good." She sighed a dreamy little sigh. "I sound like a teenager, but I don't care."

Maggie stepped back. "I think that sounds perfect."

Brooke turned around and gave Maggie a hug. "I'm gonna miss you." She glanced around the oversized bathroom that doubled as a salon. "This place has good bones, you know? Even the cabinet and mirror have personality. Sad to see it all leave your hands."

"Thank you so much."

Brooke smiled. "Please come back for a visit sometime, okay?"

"And bring my salon kit?" Maggie asked with a laugh.

"Haha—yes!"

After Brooke left and Maggie began cleaning up the *salon,* her mind idly replayed their conversation. *I sound like a teenager, but I don't care ...*

Maggie had almost wanted to respond with: *Teens know how to love, don't they?* but she'd thought better of it. Still, her mind wandered back to a place that ached to this day to think about.

"Hi," she'd whispered to Luke, the night after they had made love under a quilt made of stars. She might have gone against everything she had always promised herself, her parents, God, but there would be no regrets. She was nearly nineteen. An adult, for goodness sake. Rather her than one of those bone-thin groupies always throwing themselves at her boyfriend. Everyone knew they only wanted him for his fame and his newfound money.

But she ... she loved him. And that was worth something. Right?

He smiled, yet his eyes held something else, his pupils dilated. She tried to kiss away what she mistook for fear that they had been found out. He did not return the kiss, but instead stepped back. A lock of his salt-water-drenched hair fell onto his forehead, and when she reached up to smooth it back, he stopped her, closing his hand over hers.

She tilted her head. "What's wrong, Luke?"

He let go of her hand and took another larger step back. "I, uh, we can't do this anymore, Mags."

She narrowed her eyes. "What do you mean? What can't we do?"

Luke's eyes darted to the side, to behind her. He would not look at her. "I'm with somebody else now."

His words landed between them like a hoax that fell flat. That

was impossible. Impossible! How could he ... ? She shook her head.
"You're lying."

"I'm not."

"But ... wait."

He shoved a hand into his pocket, his chin set. "It's not like you're here all year. Things happen."

"I was in school. You knew that. And you wrote to me!"

"Yeah, well, things have changed a lot around here."

She stepped back, her eyes burning. "You mean you're famous now? And stupid girls throw themselves at you all day long?"

He didn't answer.

"You're better than that, Luke." She steadied herself, mindful of the catch in her throat and the onslaught of tears behind her eyes. "Last night was everything I ever dreamed."

He lifted his chin, his gaze cloudy. "It was a mistake."

The coldness of his words landed like ice water on her warm skin.

"You don't mean that."

He licked his lips, a flicker of sorrow quickly replaced with hard resolve. "I gotta go. See ya."

"Luke, wait!" She gripped his wrist. "What's happening? Why are you doing this?"

He spun around until his eyes were inches from her. "CeCe's pregnant."

Her gut clenched. "CeCe? That skinny blonde? You said she followed you around like an annoying cat!"

She had poked him with a fire iron. He stood to his full height and crossed his sculpted arms in front of his chest.

She continued. "How do you know it's yours?"

"I know."

"Are you ... marrying her?"

He paused before answering. "Yes."

"No." She shook her head and the tears began to slide down her cheeks. This wasn't happening. Not now. Not after all the years of waiting for each other. And not after last night. "Tell me this is all some kind of mistake."

"Can't." Luke dropped his hands to his sides.

She shook her head so hard her neck hurt. "You can't leave now."

Luke backed away, shrugging, as if that was all there was left to say. Then he spun around and stalked off, leaving Maggie alone to sweep up the mess of the relationship that he had left behind.

8

"C 'mon, Eva. Let's go or you'll be late for camp!"

Eva skidded into the living room with her beach bag over her shoulder and a pair of black sunglasses covering her eyes.

"The house too sunny for you?"

Her daughter lifted her chin and posed, like some duck-faced celebrity. "They're cool."

"Yeah, sure," Maggie said. "But only until you stub your toe because you can't see in front of yourself."

Eva giggled as she bounded from the house and onto the sand. Like her own days of summer camp, time had a way of disappearing before Maggie could digest the minutes. If she could somehow slow these years of Eva evolving from a little girl to a pre-teen, she would.

A sudden arrow of grief pierced Maggie's heart. She missed her mother something fiercely on days like today. Her mom had been her champion, even though Maggie had let her down. Instead of listening to her mother's soothing advice, she had knee-jerked her way into a detour: Two days after Luke's announcement, Maggie hitched a ride back to Arizona and right into the arms of the town bad boy, Greg. He'd been after her all through high school and, at her lowest point, she finally gave in.

Jake hadn't come to the beach house that summer, or else he probably would have decked Luke. Her sisters didn't really notice what was happening, as they were all still stuck in crushes and summertime romances of their own. But it was her mother who had pointedly urged her not to rebound with Greg.

Of course, that was before the phone call. Two weeks after that terrible day with Luke, her mother called her in Arizona to deliver the news that had seemed as final as death: Luke and CeCe had gotten married in a friend's backyard.

She shut her eyes, remembering the icy path the news made through her veins. She had been grounded in faith when she was young, and believed that marriage was for life. Her parents had modeled that, too. But despite the trouble she had suddenly found herself in—learning that she, too, was pregnant—no way would Maggie Holloway try to break up Luke's.

She groaned out loud as she relived that memory.

"Something s'matter, Mom?" Eva asked.

"What? No." Maggie shook her head quickly. "Sorry. Was just thinking about my to-do list."

"You do that a lot."

"Do not."

"Yeah. You do. Sometimes you even move your lips when you're thinking."

Maggie gasped. "Not true."

Eva stopped and put her hand on Maggie's shoulder, patting it a couple of times. "It's okay. You have a lot to think about."

They trudged along together through the sand, Segura Beach feeling farther away somehow. As Maggie's calves cramped, she slowed, but Eva ran on ahead until she was less than shouting distance. Maggie stopped and cupped a hand around her mouth. "Well, goodbye to you too, Eva!"

Eva turned a one-eighty, a crooked smile lighting her face. "Bye, Mom!"

"I'll be here when you're done!"

"Okay!" Eva flashed her a thumbs up and took off toward the water's edge.

Maggie shook her head, smiling in spite of herself. She scanned the beach for a spot where she could sit with her back to the sun while still having a wide view of the water, when Luke's voice broke her concentration. "Hi, stranger."

"Hi." Maggie cringed. She still had one foot in the memory she'd been replaying, the one full of regret that should have been long buried with no chance of being unearthed.

"You all right?"

"I am."

"Good. I was thinking of going for a walk. Want to join me?"

She hesitated, her mind still unsettled. She hadn't slept well and wondered if it would be better to refuse and just plop down onto the sand for a nap. But then she reminded herself—she and Luke had agreed to be friends. Maggie glanced out to the horizon. She wouldn't be able to see this for very much longer.

"Is that a no?"

"Sure. I mean, no." She huffed a sigh. "Yes, let's take that walk."

The tide had washed out, giving them a low, flat surface to walk across for as far as they could see. In the distance, a formation of pelicans flew close to the water's surface, far away from the shoreline, no doubt looking for fish dinner that had washed deeper into the ocean.

"Can I ask you a question?" Maggie said, longing to think about anything other than the mistakes of her past.

"Anything."

"Why don't you surf anymore? I asked you once before, but you never gave me an answer."

He slowed his pace momentarily. "I can't answer that."

"You said I could ask you anything."

"Didn't say I'd answer, though."

She crossed her arms. Why this frustrated her, she didn't know. Then she remembered: He had done this before, back when they were young. How had she forgotten how stubborn he always was?

Maybe because she was equally as stubborn ...

"Hey." He reached out to her, stopping until she looked at him.

She released a breath, gathering her thoughts. "I know it's been years since we've seen each other, really talked the way we used to, Luke. But sometimes it feels like yesterday."

He nodded. "I know."

"And yesterday, you were a champion surfer. A stubborn champion surfer."

Luke shook his head. "Not really. Just a guy with a stick."

Maggie almost smiled at his use of the old term for surfboard. She peered at him. "Why'd you quit?"

Conflict marred his face, his gaze landing nowhere.

She leaned her head to the side. "Did you think you'd fall easily for the fame again? The women?"

Luke scoffed. "Please."

"Because that's why you left the circuit, right? I mean, CeCe and Siena certainly didn't stop you, I don't think. From what I remember, CeCe was all about being with the reigning surf champ of Colibri Beach."

The words flew out of her mouth sounding far snarkier than she had planned. Not that she had planned anything ...

He looked up sharply. "This isn't worth talking about."

"Oh no?" Maggie shrugged and looked out to the lapping tide. "I guess you're right. It really was all a bunch of garbage, wasn't it, Luke? I mean, not your skills, but the fame? The popularity? Oh and all those ridiculous girls!"

"Stop." Luke grabbed her hands. He was inches from her now, his breath uneven, like he had just run up a hill. His eyes bored into hers. "What about Rafael?"

Maggie frowned. "Rafael? The guy with the ... bod?"

"Don't mess with me. I know you were with him."

Maggie recoiled. "With him ... how?"

Luke's eyes flittered all over her face now, and she couldn't decide what she desired more—to fall deeply into his embrace or smack him with everything she had. Lucky for him, she still hadn't decided.

"You went to him. The day after I told you that CeCe was pregnant. I saw you with that guy on the beach. He was ... smug."

A million, whirring thoughts circled her brain until one pulled ahead of the others. The memory hit her with clarity. Luke was right, well, sort of. Why had she blocked this memory for so long?

Rafael, ever-shirtless, had come upon her crying the night that Luke had shredded her heart. He dried her tears with the damp towel he'd carried home from the beach and she'd buried her face in his chest. It struck her now how coveted a spot that was for the girls of Colibri. But for her? Just a safe place to land.

She and Rafael had fallen asleep on the beach that night and hours later, in the early morning hours, watched as the sunrise cast a glow upon the Pacific Ocean.

Another memory rose: her dad. Her father had been livid that she had been out all night. So what if she was over eighteen? "Did you spend the night with that guy?" he'd said, nearly accusing her of something that was, to him, unthinkable.

If only he really knew all that had happened that night ...

One look at her mother, though, and the truth came out —with a bucketful of tears to wash it down. Though she didn't see it herself, she surmised that her mother had silenced her father with one hard look. And then her mother had spent the rest of the morning listening to Maggie's cries and teenaged torment over Luke's sudden predicament— and dismissal of her.

"Maggie, did you hear me?" Luke stood there, his face screwed up into some self-righteous expression.

She blinked. "Did I hear you what? Accuse me of looking for solace after you threw away everything we had?"

Luke sputtered.

How dare he throw shade at her? After what he'd done, who cared who she might have—and might *not* have—found sympathy with?

Maggie stopped in place. It didn't matter that they had traveled light years since those days of heartache and confusion. She had made the best decision she felt equipped to make at the time, the decision she thought was best for everyone, including Luke. She'd prayed. She talked it out with her mom—and Greg, and that was that.

And now, these ten years later, she had already weathered the pain of a difficult marriage and single motherhood. Maggie could hold her head up—this she knew. Her parents had trained her well. She was resilient. And she wasn't about to let anyone—even Luke Hunter—try to take that away from her.

Luke tapped his pencil repeatedly on the front counter in his shop, while Siena sat on a stool nearby, idly reading a book about a garden with secrets. She'd pulled her hair up into some kind of bun with all kinds of curls coming out of it. It looked nice.

The morning traffic had been brisk as tourist season had kicked in with full force. Guys and girls milled about, but it was the boys he wanted to corral and knock sense into. He wanted to tell them to keep a cool head when it came to girls, that he understood the rush of testosterone, the thrill of appreciation, and the victory of ... well, maybe he oughta keep some things to himself.

If he could give them one piece of advice, it was to think before acting and listen before speaking.

If only he had followed his own advice with Maggie. He hung his head and tried to focus on work. Though he continued to stare at the order sheet on the counter, he couldn't see or concentrate on any of it. He had blown it.

Again. He had asked Maggie to walk the beach, hoping to explore her feelings for him. Instead, he'd stubbornly refused to answer a question she had asked him in earnest.

And then he had spun the conversation to her choices. He rubbed the back of his neck, a simmering anger tightening his nerves. He still seethed thinking about seeing Maggie with that guy. Knowing that Maggie was forever linked to Rafael made him break out in a sweat.

"Hey, boss," Carlos said, breaking his self-loathing. "How much for the shorts?"

Luke snapped a look up, still unseeing. He squinted. "Uh. Not marked?"

"Nope."

He rubbed his eyes. "Hang on a second." Quickly he pulled the pricing sheet he kept under the counter. Old school, but it worked for him. He relayed the price to Carlos, who returned to the customer. Luke sighed. In some ways, this mental tussle over a girl who kept him from doing things as he ought to reminded him of growing up more than just about anything else.

Luke glanced at the calendar. Maggie and Eva's departure was days away, and from what he had picked up in snippets of conversation, the house would be sold as soon as summer ended. Maybe what had gone down was for the best. They could chalk up their argument to what it was: a disagreement between old friends.

But then, why did he feel like he had taken a pounding like rocks into sand?

Maybe he should tell her about his ... mishap. He rubbed the scar over his lip, bringing on a slice of phantom pain.

Luke pressed his mouth into a grim line. Some things

were not worth reliving, no matter how many times he'd heard it could be cathartic. He didn't want to take that chance. Then again, the accident led to decisions that CeCe could never accept.

Even after you got me, you wanted Maggie.

The words she spat at him after signing the divorce papers resurfaced in his consciousness, but he had to come to terms with his part, if any, in CeCe's decline. He looked across the shop to the teens in the corner watching an unending loop of surf footage on a flat screen. They could be anywhere but here today—looking at their phones, hiding under the covers, out causing trouble—but they were here. A safe place that played homage to a quintessential beach town sport.

"Dad?" Siena stared up at him, eyes sparkling.

"Hm?"

"Could you put some things on your order list for me?"

He held his smile back by pursing his lips. He had no idea what she wanted, but figured it would be something electronic. With a screen. "What is it, kiddo?"

"I need some smoothing cream for my flyaway hair. And a wet brush."

"A *wet* brush?"

"You know, for brushing my hair when it's wet so it won't get all tangly. Oh, and could you get me a bag of elastics so I can braid my hair?"

He grinned. His little surf girl never seemed to do anything but shake her wet hair after a shower or time in the ocean. A pang of regret caught him in the windpipe, his smile fading. Maybe he should have investigated what was out there for her. Never crossed his mind.

"Sure, honey. I'll add those things to my order when I'm online later."

"You could always ask Maggie for help," she said, with a shrug. "She knows stuff about that."

Maggie. Of course. Siena had been spending so much time over at the Holloway house that she'd picked up some tips from the hairstylist of the family. Maybe from Eva, too.

Luke turned slightly so Siena could not see emotion building on his face. Maybe it was time to stop blaming himself for CeCe's ... disappointment. He'd done the very best he could with few instructions. Now, he had the chance to right some wrongs for both him—and for Siena.

Friendship was a start, but Luke knew he wanted something more with Maggie. He determined to tell her—and soon.

MAGGIE SPENT the next few days on the phone. In between trimming Lea's bangs, washing and setting Wren's hair, and touching up paint all over the beach house, she had finalized a rental apartment in exactly the place she wanted to be. The complex had a pool, laundry, a workout room (woo-hoo!), and it was walking distance to Eva's school. Well, a long walk, but still.

She owed undying gratitude to Jake, who had agreed to co-sign for her. He had, of course, offered to just buy the whole darn building—she was sure that was said in jest—but independence was important to Maggie. Not just for herself, but she also wanted to model that for Eva.

And best of all, she had an interview with an absolutely

perfect salon with tons of walk-in traffic right near downtown. As the days sped toward Lacy's arrival, everything was falling into place. Bella should have been the one to take her month at the house, but she couldn't get away from work. Who knew selling essential oils was so lucrative? Thankfully, Lacy had agreed to step in. Maggie's shoulders relaxed just thinking about it—Lacy didn't relent on hardly anything. She would stage the house and Bella would do the final deep clean.

It had all been decided.

She eyed the bathroom cabinet, thankful that Jake had decided to leave it when he updated the room. Like just about everyone had commented, it was a beautiful piece and she held a fleeting thought, hoping that the future owners would not discard it. And knowing they probably would.

Maggie sighed. She bent down on her haunches and flung open the doors. Inside was surprisingly clean, though the contact paper her mother used had faded beyond recognition. She reached in, pulling out old cleaning solutions, wayward sponge rollers—they reminded her of her mother —and pried a few bobby pins off of the cabinet's floor. A curled up slip of paper was beyond her grasp, so she stretched as hard as she could to retrieve it. The surface felt rough in her hands. She pulled it out and sat back on her heels.

"Eva? Come here!" Maggie called down the hall.

"What's up?"

"Look." Maggie held up the uncurled document to her.

Eva took it and scrunched her face. "Ew. What is this?"

Maggie reached for it and took a long look at it again. "I think it's supposed to be you and a cat."

"Doesn't look like a cat. Why's all that glitter on it?"

"Well, it was your three-year-old version of one. And the glitter's there because you loved the stuff."

"Me?"

Maggie laughed, feeling it deep down to her core. "You made it for Grandma and I sent it to her."

Eva laughed a little. "I guess she didn't like it very much since she hid it in that cabinet."

"Oh contraire! She loved your drawings. I bet she loved this one especially because you made it just for her. And ..."

"And what?"

"Well, you really, really, REALLY wanted her to buy you a kitty cat."

"I don't like them much anymore."

Maggie snickered. "I know."

Eva looked at the picture again. She threw her head back suddenly and exhaled a high-pitched laugh. "This cat sorta looks like a man—look at its big nose!"

Maggie smiled, though she felt a check of something inside of her. Eva's laugh, the one she'd heard many times, was reminiscent of ... Luke's laugh. Why hadn't she noticed it before?

Eva shook her head and began walking away. "I was a weird kid, Mom."

Still on her knees, Maggie leaned through the doorway and called down the hall after her daughter. "Not true!" Eva continued that high-pitched laughter even as she traipsed back to her room.

Maggie closed her eyes and rolled onto her bum. She leaned against the wall and looked more closely at the drawing, an old memory coming into view. Was this a drawing of a cat? Or ... a man? Somewhere in the watery past, she recalled Eva asking about her father. Greg had been long gone by then, chased away by his own inability to make good on his promise.

She heard Eva's three-year-old voice in her head. "This is me, mommy."

"And who is that with you?"

Eva thought. "He's my ... daddy! I put glitter on him!"

Maggie returned to the present and shut her eyes, moisture and heat building behind them. Small similarities between Eva and Luke rolled through her mind like an old film strip. The way they both liked pistachio ice cream. Yuck, by the way. The on-off curb hopping when they walked down the sidewalk. And that silly laugh. She hung her head, trying not to hyperventilate.

Of course, some of her sisters laughed like that, especially when tipsy. So maybe that wasn't exactly an indicator of his parentage? Oh ... but that dark hair. Between hair bleach and the sun's own natural lightening powers, even she had been fooled. She huffed out a sarcastic laugh, wondering why it had never occurred to her how much Eva favored Luke.

She knew she was leaving, but somehow, it felt premature. But what had she thought would happen when she came schlepping back to town with her sweet daughter? Surely people could do the math and at least suspect that Luke was Eva's father.

Her sisters hadn't, though. As far as she knew. Neither had Jake.

Maggie groaned out a sigh. For just a moment, she imagined life as it could be if unencumbered by a secret. And a lie. And past hurts.

Despite the cost, Maggie realized, it was time—past time —to tell Luke the truth. She had to. She pulled herself up to her feet and glanced into the mirror, her expression mottled with uncertainty. Telling Luke was the right thing to do. But in doing so, she could lose him forever. Again.

She would have to take that chance.

MAYBE HE SHOULD HAVE CALLED FIRST. Luke stood on the front porch of the Holloway house, reliving his childhood. How many times had he stood in this very place, his hair combed back, his posture straight, and knocked on the old wooden screen door? Maggie's dad could severely injure a guy's spirit with one bend of his evil, fatherly gaze. In some ways, he had the man to thank for his ability to look his elders in the eye and carry on a decent conversation.

He rapped on the door with his knuckles.

Eva appeared and attempted to peer past him. "Hi Luke. Is Siena with you?"

Why hadn't he thought about the fact that what he wanted to talk about would have to be done in private?

"Hey, Eva. Sorry—not this time."

She shrugged. "You want to come in?"

"Yes, if your mom's here."

She opened the door wide and stood back. "She's in the bathroom."

Luke stopped. "I'll wait, uh, in the living room."

Eva quirked a look up at him. A smile dawned on her

face, followed by raucous, contagious laughter. "It's 'cause she's been painting it!"

"Oh. Right."

Eva rolled her eyes, still laughing. "Come on. I'll show you."

He followed by Eva, who skipped down the hall. They found Maggie standing in the large bathroom staring into space. She yelped when he appeared in the doorway.

"Sorry if I scared you," Luke said. He noticed the drawn, pale expression on her face. "Busy?"

She put a palm to her chest, as if steadying herself. "I-I'm —no. Not anymore. Was just thinking about you, actually."

He leaned his head to the side, lowering his voice. "Really?"

"Yes."

Luke sent a quick glance down the hall, aware of how voices carried. "It's a perfect day outside. Want to check it out?"

"Luke Hunter, when is it never a perfect day at the beach?"

He laughed gently. "I hear you. But"—he slid his gaze toward the open doorway—"was thinking maybe we could talk in private."

Maggie nodded, though he noticed a momentary hesitation. They headed down the hall and toward the back porch, his mind toggling between how different today was compared to the many times he had taken this same walk as a teen.

Maggie put her hand on the door and turned back. "Eva? Luke and I'll be outside."

Eva called back, "Okay!"

Outside, trails of clouds stretched across the sky, translucent enough to let sunlight pour through. The old tattered umbrella that the Holloway family once had on this porch was long gone, as was most of the furniture, save a couple of rickety chairs and Mrs. Holloway's old pink bench. It struck Luke how much he missed the way things were.

He leaned his forearms on the wooden rail, glad that it had been pummeled smooth over time. "Do you remember when we used to get up early and go out to the sand?"

"Hm. I do. Was fun. A whole bunch of us would do it—even Lacy, sometimes. My dad yelled at me one year when he realized that our sleeping bags were heavy because they were full of sand."

Luke laughed. "I'd forgotten about the sleeping bags!"

"That's because you were out in the surf." She shook her head. "I was always so proud of you for getting out there so early. I couldn't do it."

"Hence, the sleeping bag on the beach."

Her mouth curled into a small smile. "It was cold."

"Life wasn't very complicated back then, was it?"

Maggie sighed, like she was thinking.

Luke eyed her. "Was that me waxing poetic?"

She laughed lightly. "I haven't heard anyone use that term since my mom. She read a lot of books."

"My mom did too."

"Ah. But to your question, yes, life was less complicated when we were here, but the rest of the time it was pretty unusual."

Dawning came over him. "Like when you guys lost your full-time home in the fire."

"Yes. And my dad's struggle with finding work." She

shrugged. "We had a good life growing up, but it seemed frenetic at times. So I know what you mean. We were lucky to have this place to come to in the summers. Not many kids get that."

"And now?"

"And now ... what?"

He turned and leaned his back on the rail so he could see her better. Man, how he loved looking at her. "What do you want your life to look like, Mags?"

She furrowed her brow, as if he had asked her a trick question, and the way she wrinkled her freckle-covered nose wasn't lost on him. "I want it to be ... simpler."

It wasn't what he had expected her to say, and yet what she wanted made so much sense. He, too, wanted a simpler life. To some, his might have looked like just that: quiet beachside community, a thriving business, a child to love.

Still, he craved more.

Luke pushed off the railing and captured Maggie's hand in his. He rubbed his thumb over that soft place between her thumb and forefinger, reveling in her warmth. "I want that too, Mags."

She snapped a look up at him, her eyes meeting his head on, a certain vulnerability in them.

"Stay here," he said.

Her gaze turned questioning. "Here? You mean, in Colibri?"

"Yes."

"Eva needs stability and I think once we, uh, reestablish ourselves in Arizona, she'll have that."

"You could do that here, Mags. I'll help you."

Instead of relief, she continued to watch him with trepidation, as if she didn't trust him. He frowned. "Hey, look, Maggie, I owe you an apology. I'm sorry for what I said about you and ... Rafael." Just saying the guy's name put a bad taste in his mouth. "It was careless of me."

Maggie sighed. She leaned into him, suddenly wrapping her arms around him, her mouth tantalizingly close to his neck. "I forgive you," she said, the heat of her breath sending a shiver through him.

"Then stay."

"I-I can't."

Luke closed his eyes, frustrated as much at his inability to tell her how he felt as he was with her steadfast plans to leave here soon. He leaned his forehead against hers. "Is it because of ... Rafael?"

Maggie leaned back, searching his face. "Are you still on that subject?"

"Well, I mean, he's sort of still in the picture. Right?"

She scrunched her forehead. "Rafael was *never* in the picture."

"Is that because he doesn't ... know?"

"Know?"

Luke rubbed his lips together, aware of the dangerous territory he had entered. Maggie had seemed closed to the subject of Rafael every time he had mentioned him, but he moved forward, undeterred. If they were going to forge a relationship that could withstand storms, they had to be honest with each other.

"Does Rafael know that he's Eva's father?"

Maggie gasped.

"I know the truth, Mags."

She narrowed her eyes. "What are you talking about?"

"I did the math. You were with him that night that I told you about CeCe being pregnant."

"You mean I *slept* with him?"

He exhaled. "You know how this town is, Mags. Someone saw you guys and, well, they didn't keep it to themselves."

She dipped her chin and shook her head. "I don't believe this." She shot a look up at him. "This is why you hate Rafael so much?"

"I don't hate people, but yeah, I don't like that guy."

"And yet, you're suggesting I stay here to live a simple life. How exactly do you see that working, Luke? In Arizona, people aren't talking about me behind my back. And certainly not about things that happened years ago. People move on." She stared at him, her eyes ablaze. "Which is exactly what I plan to do."

Luke reached for her. "Hold on a second ..."

Maggie wrested herself away from him, her breathing pronounced. She zeroed in on him, her voice low. "You were my first, Luke. How dare you assume that I ... that I would throw myself in the arms of someone I didn't care about like —like you did."

Luke's jaw tightened.

Maggie's eyes glistened, causing something in his gut to twist. "In case you've forgotten, I married Greg. He didn't turn out to be the man I'd hoped for. Actually, none of the men I've met have, so that's on me to learn to choose better." She moved toward the back door but stopped short. A tear dripped down her cheek. "But don't try to make me out to be as tawdry as *you*."

Luke exhaled harshly as he closed the space between

them. He reached for her hand and took it in his, saying, "Maggie, are you really never going to forgive me?"

Her shoulders rose and fell with each jagged breath, her expression more drawn than when he had first come upon her in the master bath. "There's nothing to forgive, Luke. We both made our choices"—she shrugged, resignation in her face—"and now we've got to find a way to live with them."

She walked into the house and shut the back door behind her, leaving Luke alone on the deck.

10

Maggie took a last twirl around the beautiful kitchen her brother had designed for the old house. She was going to miss it.

"Knock, knock." Daisy entered the house, a basket in her hands.

"Hey."

"Hey, yourself." She plunked the basket on the island. "My mother made you an apple pie and sliced it so you could eat it on the road."

"You're kidding."

Daisy shook her head, her ponytail swishing behind her. "No, I am not. She worked all day on it yesterday."

"That is the sweetest thing I've ever heard."

"No pun intended."

Maggie smiled. "Ha. Don't my hips know it. I really should go over and thank her."

"She's down for a long nap, so don't worry about that. I'll tell her that both you and your hips thank her."

Maggie laughed outright now and pulled Daisy into a hug. "Gonna miss you, girl."

"Same."

Eva traipsed into the room wearing a dour expression. "Hi, Aunt Daisy. Momma, can I go to the beach one more time?"

Maggie sighed. "Okay. Yes. But stay in sight. We're leaving soon."

When Eva had gone back down the hall, Daisy tilted her head in Maggie's direction, a question in her eyes. "I know you're not thrilled about leaving, but I have to ask—is there something wrong?"

"How can you tell?"

Daisy shrugged. "Not sure, really. You look sad, though. Can I help?"

"No, not really." Maggie licked her lips, her eyes downcast. She needed a friend right now, but couldn't fathom unlocking the secret that had been in a vault for all these years, though she had planned to do just that yesterday. Until Luke accused her of a relationship with ... Rafael.

Maggie glanced again at Daisy. "The truth is, Luke and I had a fight."

"Oh. Were you and he, I mean—?"

"No. We're not together. But he said something that upset me and it's been gnawing at me. He basically thought that I, uh, had been with Rafael."

Daisy's eyes popped open. "You mean, like, slept with him?"

"Yes." She frowned. "Not now, but a long time ago. Not sure why I let it bother me so much, but it did. We weren't here all the time as kids, but living here as an adult has been eye-opening. Lots of gossip, you know."

"Yes, I know. Doesn't help when the local realtor seems to like to spread it around."

Maggie nodded.

Daisy was quiet a moment. "You know, your brother just about split his mind thinking I had something going on with Rafael."

"You're kidding."

"Nope."

"That's ... hilarious. Sort of."

"What is? That I might have been having a fling with Rafael or that your brother wasn't taking it well?"

"That second part."

Daisy laughed. "Yes, well, he didn't find it funny. At all."

Maggie leaned forward. "Does Rafael still run around without a shirt on? I mean, I saw him once on the beach since I got here, but, you know, is it still a regular thing with him?"

Daisy giggled. "Yes, ma'am."

"Shew."

"Yeah, girl. I was immune to his charms, though. He's always been a friend, a real sweetheart, so that's how I thought of him while he was walking around my mom's place all glossy and wearing a tool belt."

"I'm surprised you didn't have an audience every day."

"I did—Jake."

Maggie smiled, genuinely. She could feel it to her toes, suddenly immensely thankful for Daisy's visit.

"You gonna be okay?" Daisy asked.

Maggie nodded. "Definitely."

With reluctance on her face, Daisy headed toward the front door. "Don't be a stranger. If you want to come back, you can always stay with my mom and me."

"Until the wedding, that is."

"Right. After that, you can stay with my mom and her caregiver. Or come down to Los Angeles ..."

Maggie laughed and hugged her sister-in-law's neck. "Don't worry. I'll let you guys be newlyweds for a while. Here," she said, opening the door. "I'll walk out with you and then go find Eva at the beach."

Together they walked between the two houses, the pound of the surf breaking up their conversation. They said their goodbyes, then Daisy continued on as Maggie stopped and scanned the beach. She frowned, unable to spot Eva.

"Want me to help you find her?" Daisy called out.

Maggie hesitated. Eva had probably just wandered out of sight.

Daisy didn't wait for her answer and jogged back to join Maggie. "C'mon. I'll go with you. I want to give her a quick hug before you two take off anyway."

Maggie slipped her shoes off and tossed them toward the house. Together she and Daisy began trudging through the sand, which was dotted with early beachgoers who had already staked their spot for the day. A few umbrellas had popped up too, reminding Maggie of what Luke had said about the tattered one she had used every summer.

Waves crashed onto the shore, interrupted only by the buzz of a small plane overhead and the occasional burst of young voices. Maggie stopped, put her hand above her eyes, and searched the beach. Daisy looked north, as Maggie squinted toward the south.

"Could she have already gone in the house through the back porch?" Daisy asked.

"Maybe." A commotion broke out near a group of people hovering around an umbrella. Maggie craned her neck, watching. A woman was waving her arms and two young boys had joined her, all three of them looking and pointing out to sea.

"Maggie?" Daisy said, her tone eerily still, "Is that Eva in the water?"

A small figure clung to a boogie board. Maggie squinted. A second figure was next to the first. Siena? "Oh no." Maggie sprinted toward the shoreline. She pointed at a pile of clothing and shoes left on the sand. "Those are Eva's." She waved her arms in the air, barely able to hear the girls' yells. Were they laughing? Or crying for help?

"Eva! Come back!"

Daisy caught up to her, her phone in her hand. "I'm calling 9-1-1 now."

"Wait. I think they're just horsing around."

"Maggie, that's a riptide they're in!"

Maggie gasped. Something in her chest twisted, the effect of it like cutting off her oxygen. "No! Eva! Siena!" She swung her arm in an arc, waving them in. "Come in!"

Daisy hung up the phone and touched Maggie's arm. She took her hands and faced her. "Listen to me. It's better that they not fight the current. They'll get too tired doing that. Remember that they have boogie boards to hang onto!"

Maggie shook her head, eyes wide, dread disabling her ability to speak.

"Try not to worry, Maggie! The fire department is on its way. Let's keep track of the girls, okay?"

"Can the fire department do water rescues?"

Daisy's brows dipped. "They-they're trying to get ahold of their rescue crew. They said they would call the lifeguard division ..."

"Oh no." Maggie sucked in a harsh breath. "I've got to call Luke."

Daisy nodded quickly. "Yes. Hurry and call him. Tell him to bring his board."

The minutes stretched after she phoned Luke, desperately relaying the girls' plight. As they waited for help, Maggie and Daisy kept their eyes focused on the girls, watching in horror as they were dragged farther down the beach.

"Dear Lord," she prayed aloud, "please, please ... please take care of the girls!"

"What in the world, Maggie!"

She spun around.

Luke ran toward her, sweat droplets on his forehead and a board under his arm. Another guy was with him. "Why did you let them go out there?"

"I didn't know!"

Luke's jaw was set. He flicked his chin toward the guy next to him. "Carlos and I are going out there."

Maggie nodded, worry turning her veins cold. Luke looked pale to her, and she knew that he, too, was feeling the strain of fear. Guilt wrapped its way around her lungs. Luke needed to know the truth about Eva, but now was not the time.

Quickly, Luke secured a leash to his ankle and picked up the board. Luke began to run toward the ocean, but then he wavered and stopped.

Maggie watched in horror as Luke bent over at the waist, put his hand on his knee, and vomited on the sand.

EVER SINCE THE day that Siena first jumped on a board the year before, Luke knew he would have to face his fears. If he'd had his wits about him, he would've closed up shop and moved inland at the first sign of Siena's interest in surfing. He had done his best to warn her about the dangers of the water, especially at this curve of the beach. "This is why surf camp is held so far to the north," he had told her.

Had he been as explicit with Maggie and Eva?

When he saw Maggie's number on his cell phone, he had been relieved. Maybe she'd had a change of heart, he thought. He picked it up on one ring.

"Luke! The girls are in trouble! You have to come quickly!"

It was the last thing he had expected her to say. Luke's heart tore at him as he jogged through the sand, his board under his arm. He found Maggie clutching an arm to her stomach, as if in pain. In the distance the girls bobbed on the water, clinging to their boards, quickly being pulled farther out to sea.

He reached down and strapped the Velcro band to his ankle, securing the leash to himself and his own stomach roiled. Luke pressed on. Siena and Eva needed him. He took a couple of steps, but an indescribable wave overtook him and his gut wretched just before his morning breakfast came up for another visit. He coughed it out, sputtering, then wiped his mouth with the back of his hand.

Maggie appeared next to him. "Luke!"

He turned to her, fighting the tide of unease.

"Oh my—Luke, are you still afraid of the water? That's why you quit, isn't it?"

His eyes bored into hers, his mouth dry and raw. She knew about his fear as a child, how it had landlocked him for years, while other kids took to the waves like dolphins.

Maggie turned her attention to the waves that Carlos had already plunged into. A small audience had gathered at the water's edge. She elicited a small whimper and his heart twisted even more.

Pastor Miguel came up on the scene and put a firm hand on Luke's shoulder. "You've got this, son."

Luke nodded. He hitched the board up under his arm and he began to run, his feet landing in cold, salty water. He tossed the board down, the sucking sound of it familiar. He jumped on and paddled out hard after Carlos, who had nearly reached Siena. The memory of the last time he'd surfed, of the day that had brought back home for him his longstanding fears, faded as he focused on the little girl holding onto her board like a champ.

Just beyond Carlos and Siena, he took in the determination on Eva's face. Her brow furrowed, her hands wrapped tightly around the edges of her board, even as water washed over her. Something about the way she tucked her chin and focused on him made his heart swell and his arms paddle faster. He had to get to her before that board got away from her.

"Eva! Hold on! Almost there!"

Water lapped over the top of his board, obstructing his

view of her. He spit out sea water, the saltiness of it tasting like his youth. "Hang on! Almost there!"

When he reached Eva, that determined gaze she'd been wearing faltered. "Luke!"

"You're going to have to let go of the board, Eva."

She shook her head. "I can't."

"Trust me." He reached his arm out and she eyed it, gritting her teeth. He was next to her now, and she grabbed onto his arm, letting her boogie board be taken away with the surf. With one strong move, he pulled her onto his board. "Just lay down flat on your stomach, Eva, and hold on tight. I'm going to get us home."

She nodded and did what he said.

"That's my girl."

Quickly, he paddled parallel to the shoreline, with Carlos and Siena following closely behind. When they had all escaped the clutches of the rip current, they turned the noses of their boards toward the beach and paddled home.

When they landed on the shore, his adrenaline still pumping, he scooped up Eva who'd gone limp from exhaustion. Her long hair had become tangled into a mass, exposing the lower part of her neck. Luke squinted, spotting a heart-shaped birthmark below her ear.

His own heart thudded erratically, pounding in his ears. He had a similar birthmark on his neck. So did Siena.

Maggie appeared, breathless, tears flowing. Eva spun out of his arms and into Maggie's mama bear embrace. Carlos brought Siena to Luke, and he lunged for her, his arms wrapping tightly around her. "What were you two thinking?" he whispered harshly into her hair.

"I'm sorry, Daddy."

Discipline would come later. Right now, he was beyond grateful that he and Carlos had gotten to the girls before tragedy could strike.

He exhaled, the adrenaline flowing out of him until fatigue, followed by realization, overcame him.

Eva broke free of her mother and ran toward Siena. "That was crazy!"

Siena turned and put out both hands until Eva grabbed hold of them. "Oh my gosh, I *know!!*"

Maggie took a step toward the girls, but Luke shot out his arm, stopping her. "I need to talk to you."

She shook her head. "Not now."

He put his hand on her arm. "Yes. Now."

Maggie turned to him, startled.

Daisy looked from Maggie to Luke. She cut in. "How about I take the girls back to the house and get them started on a shower, hm?"

Maggie nodded her okay.

Carlos glanced at his father next to him before turning his attention back to Luke. He cleared his throat. "If it's all right with you, boss, I'm gonna head back."

Luke gave him a fist bump. "Thanks, man. You were awesome. I owe you big."

"Nah. They're safe now, so I got my reward."

When they were left there in the silence punctuated only by the call of birds and stray children, Luke stared at Maggie. Last night, he had planned to tell her how he felt about her, that he loved her—and that he always had. But now? He wanted the truth, and he wasn't going to leave here without it.

"She's mine, isn't she? Eva is ... mine."

Maggie shrank back, her eyes big, wide. Finally, she whispered, "Yes."

He sucked on his top lip, shaking his head. "And you were just going to leave here today with that little secret, weren't you?"

"I was going to tell you last night."

"I don't believe you."

"It's true."

"Then why didn't you?"

She paused. "I don't know."

"You've had years to tell me this, Maggie. Years!"

She shook her head. "It's more complicated than that, Luke."

"Enlighten me. You owe me that, at least."

Maggie hugged herself around the middle and lowered herself into the sand. She burrowed her feet down deep. When she looked up at him, her eyes were like gray clouds. "I found out I was pregnant after moving home. By then, I was dating Greg. I mean, he'd wanted me to date him all through high school, but I never did because"—she shrugged—"well, because I loved you, Luke."

She continued, "After you dumped me, he helped to tape up my heart as best he could. And when I found out I was pregnant, he said he wanted to marry me and be a father to my baby. So we got married."

Luke's jaw was set. "Why didn't you tell me?"

The rising sun settled on her face. "My mother asked me not to. She said you were happily married already and that it wouldn't be right to do that to you, to be a home wrecker. Plus, there was Greg to consider. He knew the baby was yours."

"How?"

She swallowed before saying, "I hadn't been with anyone else, Luke. Only you."

Luke sucked in a breath.

"Greg made me promise not to tell anyone. He said he would be Eva's dad as long as I didn't tell anybody about you. I think he didn't want anyone to think of him as second best."

"I see."

"I never meant to hurt you, Luke. Or Eva. I did what I thought was best at the time. But hindsight is, well, at least twenty-forty."

The corner of his mouth quirked upward. He thought about her story and about his. If only she had been honest with him, maybe things could have been different.

"When I came back here, I hoped to keep our distance. I didn't know about CeCe's problems. For all I knew, you were still a happily married guy and I was just here to fulfill my parents' wishes. In, out, and keep my distance—that's what I had planned."

"But you didn't."

"Not on purpose, and I think you know that." Maggie released a small groan. "I'd forgotten how small this town was, Luke."

He shrugged. "It's not all bad. People around here know about CeCe and they've stayed quiet for Siena's sake."

"Did you love her?"

He hesitated. "She gave me Siena."

Maggie nodded her understanding.

"Marrying her was a mistake, but I was committed to making it work."

"Yes. Of course." She lifted her chin, her eyes wide as she searched his face. In them, he saw pools of regret. "Can you ever forgive me, Luke?"

Luke stepped back, overwhelmed by the conflicting thoughts in his head. His heart pleaded with him, but his head would not back down. "You kept her from me, Maggie. I'm not sure that I ever can."

11

I did what I thought was best at the time.

For the past four days, Luke had been living in a fog. He'd slept, awakened, gone to work, and parented Siena in one of those gray haze-like moods that left zero room for light. Maggie's revelation had sent him into a spiral that he hadn't yet been able to spit himself out of, and he was beginning to wonder if he ever could. Except for Maggie's thin explanation—and the truth that Eva was his daughter—he had not thought about much else.

Luke rubbed the scar above his lip, remembering. He still didn't speak about the day that had ended his brief run at championship surfing, but yesterday's water rescue had brought it back to him in colorful clarity. He never thought he would have the desire again to get back into that water, but seeing Siena and Eva caught in a riptide?

He would jump into that sea all over again to save them.

Tension rippled through his chest. What if he had lost Siena? He couldn't bear to consider it. And Eva? He had already lost her once—he knew that now. The realization that he could have lost her a second time was more than he could fathom.

Luke's stomach churned. Would he ever get past the news and happenings of the past day?

"Hey, Dad? Did I get my shipment?"

Luke lifted his chin. He looked at Siena, but didn't truly see her. "Sorry?"

"You know, my hair stuff?"

Luke pursed his lips. Finally, he said, "You're going to have to give me more than that."

Siena let out a drama-filled sigh and put her hands on her hips. "Daddy, didn't you order me some smoothing cream and a wet brush? And the elastics?"

"Right. Yes." He rummaged through a stack of packages and plucked a large envelope from the bunch. "Forgot all about that."

Siena squealed and took the package from him. She ripped it open and emptied the contents onto the counter. "I'm so happy! This is gonna help me with my flyaway hair so I can do stuff after surfing."

Luke's chin jerked up. She wanted to get back into the water? He looked over at the products on the counter, noting the freebie samples that had been included. "You know how to use all this?"

"Dad," she said, her tone admonishing, "haven't you noticed the way I've been braiding my hair and stuff?"

His eyes connected with hers and he shifted a glance to her hair. He *had* noticed something was different ...

Siena rolled her eyes. "Men!"

"Hey." Luke reached over the counter and hooked his

arm around the back of Siena's neck. Then he kissed her on the head. "I love your hair no matter what you do with it."

"Da-ad!"

He chuckled, glad for the break in his otherwise surly mood.

Siena scooped up all the hair stuff and climbed off the stool. "Is it okay if I go show Maggie and Eva?"

He shut his eyes, trying to calm the cacophony in his brain.

"Are you okay?"

"I'm fine, Siena." His eyes were open now and he was taking her in. Siena was growing up, and for the first time ever, he saw glimpses of the young woman she was becoming. He put on a smile. "Sure. But don't stay long—and don't go near the water today, you hear me?"

Siena skipped out of the surf shop with that bag of stuff under her arm just as Zach came buzzing into the shop. "Hey, bossman!"

"Hey yourself, bud. What's up?"

"Ringer Surf Classic, that's what." The kid dumped a stack of fliers on the counter. "These are leftovers. Can I leave 'em?"

Luke lifted a brow. "I don't know. Are you telling your boss that you've spread them all over town?"

"Hey, I ain't lyin'. Dude, these are seriously leftovers. I've put 'em up on all the stores around here except that old real estate place."

"She shut you down, huh?"

"Yeah. She said Colibri oughta be hosting more dignified events, like upscale car shows and wine tastin's."

Luke snorted. "Of course she did."

"She has these super sharp claws."

"Change of subject. How's the talent shaping up for the contest? All levels filled?"

Zack shrugged. "Guess so. Did I tell you I saw her pick her nose with one of her claws?"

Luke scrunched up his forehead. "You still talking about Ms. Madsen?"

Zack's face split into a huge grin. "Yeah."

Luke grabbed the stack of fliers and knocked Zack on the head with them. "Stop it. Be respectful."

"'k." Zack cracked up on the way out of the shop.

A sharp whistle caught Luke's attention. He looked toward Carlos. "Yo!"

"Dude wants a longer leash for his board. You have any left?"

Luke ducked down and rummaged through a box under the counter. One of these days he was going to take some time and reorganize the place. He put his hands on one and then called out across the shop, "Catch it!"

It landed in Carlos's outstretched hand just as Siena wandered back into the shop, her expression downcast. Luke watched her snake through the busy shop, her brow furrowed. She climbed up on a stool, set her stuff on the counter, and leaned her cheek into her hand.

"What's up? Eva not home?" He still had so much to unpack there, but for the moment, he kept his focus on Siena.

"Nope. They left."

A rod of heat shoved its way down his back. "Left? You mean, they're not at the house right now?"

Siena shrugged both shoulders. "Eva's aunt said they went back home."

"Home?"

"Yeah. Back to Arizona, Dad."

THE LAST TIME Luke stood on this porch, things didn't go very well. But he was determined that, this time, he wouldn't mess things up.

Then again, what had his pastor said? *Be careful not to keep revisiting what the Lord has released you from.*

After much prayer and discussion, he realized he'd been wallowing in his failures, and not accepting the healing and restoration that had been offered him.

And it was time to stop.

He knocked again and a tall brunette answered the door to the Holloway home. She wore her hair pulled back into a severe ponytail and lasered her dark eyes on him, her ruby red lips twisted into a salacious grin.

"My," she said. "It looks like I might enjoy this one-horse town more than I had imagined."

"I'm looking for Maggie."

The woman huffed a laugh. "Won't I do?"

"Lacy?"

"Guilty."

He stuck his tongue hard against his cheek. "Luke Hunter."

She pushed open the screen door and looked him over from head to toe. "Hi, Stringbean."

Luke tried to hold his rising anxiety in check. He planted both feet wide, arms crossed. "Where'd she go?"

Lacy shrugged, her eyes dancing, that mouth of hers playing games. She hadn't changed a bit since they were kids. "Her month was up, so she left. Back to the desert and all her hair products and drudgery. Can I help you with something?"

He began to back away, then stopped. "Yes. You can tell me where to find her."

12

"Eva! C'mon, honey. I have to meet the owner of the salon in a few minutes. Don't make me late!"

Eva stomped into the living room of their sparse apartment. There hadn't been time to empty the storage unit nor hire a moving truck to bring in the heavy things. It would be a while before Maggie could afford all that, so for now, they were making do with a shared bed, a coffee table for meals—and that's about it.

But, seriously, it was summer. What more did they need but their clothes and somewhere to rest at night?

Eva stood with a frown and her arms folded in front of her. "Why can't I just stay here?"

Maggie washed a gaze over her. Her daughter was nearly eleven, going on twenty-five. So much had happened in the last month that she'd barely had time to download it all, let alone explain it to her child. The past few days had been a particular whirlwind and she almost couldn't believe that they were here already and living their new life. Well, almost living it.

"I want your opinion of the salon," Maggie lied. It wasn't a complete lie. She did hope that Eva would feel comfortable coming to the new salon after school, and that the others would welcome her there. Like they had in the old place.

A knock on her door startled her. Grrr! The new landlord had already shown up three times to fix things that should have been taken care of before they had moved in. *She didn't have time for this!*

Maggie swung open the door, prepared to be firm but kind. She had an interview to get to and nobody was going to stop her.

"Hello, Maggie."

Luke?

"May I come in?"

She hesitated. Yes, they had something to discuss, but when it came to the two of them, he had made himself clear: he would not forgive her. Maggie leaned her bum against the doorframe and crossed her arms at her middle. "I have a job interview in ten minutes, Luke. This is not a good time."

Eva squeezed in between the frame and the open door. "Hi, Luke! Is Siena here too?"

Luke broke away from Maggie's gaze to take in Eva, who stood there gaping at him. "Sorry, kiddo, she's not. But hopefully we'll all be together again soon."

Maggie gave her head a tight shake. "Really, Luke. I can't right now."

"I can't believe you just left."

Maggie slid a glance to Eva. "We, uh, our month was up

and I have to get back to work. Besides, I thought we had said all that needed saying."

"Sorry. Nope."

Eva shook her head. "Yeah, Mom. Sorry. Nope."

Maggie gave her daughter "the look" before directing a sobering expression at Luke. "You came a long way for nothing."

He broke out into a smile, his eyes never losing hers. "Just the opposite. I came a long way for everything."

Maggie stared at him for a good, long while. When she was done staring at him, she nodded at Eva. "Go to your room, please."

Eva's mouth opened in protest, but Luke winked at her. "Probably a good idea. Don't worry. I won't leave without you." He slid his gaze to Maggie. "Right?"

Eva yelped and scampered off, shutting a door behind her.

Luke quirked a confident smile at Maggie. He took a step forward and put one hand on the door. "May I?" He barely waited for an answer and stepped inside.

Maggie continued to hug her middle as she stepped back. "Listen, Luke, I know—"

"You don't know anything." He stepped so close that she could feel his warm breath on her face. Luke's hands found her cheeks, his fingers nestled in her hair, stopping her retreat. "Mags," he whispered. "I've missed you."

Warning flags shot up in her brain, but she ignored them. His gentle touch sent shocking waves of longing through her. She dared to wonder if this moment could possibly last. With effort, she lifted her chin and her eyes searched his. "Why are you here?"

"I want Eva to know who I am."

Her momentary high lessened some. "Of course. I-I didn't intend to hide her away from you, Luke. As I told you the other day, I fully intended to tell you the truth."

Luke held two fingers to her lips. "Sshh. I wasn't finished. I want you, Maggie. I *need* you."

A silent beat fell between them and Maggie lowered her gaze.

He pulled her closer, slowly tipping her chin up.

She searched his eyes. "What changed?"

"Nothing. Everything." Luke enveloped her with his arms. His lips grazed her cheek as she let her eyes fall closed again. "Siena started doing her hair. She had me buy all kinds of things I've never heard of—all because a woman named Maggie cared enough to show her what to do."

Maggie could feel the tears pushing through and she forced herself to let him see her. "She's a precious girl, Luke."

He pulled back, his eyes searching her face. "Here's the thing: She's CeCe's daughter as much as mine. And yet, you cared for her the way her own mother never would. Even when it was her birth that broke us up, you didn't treat her any differently than your own daughter." His gaze continued to wash over her, sending chills throughout her body. "I've been a dolt."

"A dolt?"

He grinned. "My mother used to say that about my dad when he wouldn't listen to her."

Maggie laughed in spite of herself. Her own parents' relationship stood the test of decades, even though they, too, called each other out now and again.

"I want to be honest with you, Maggie." He tapped his

upper lip with his fingertip. "You see this scar? This little beauty ended my surfing career."

"I've wondered about it."

"Happened one unhappy day when I'd tackled waves I had no business going after. Did it anyway and the board got away from me. Came down on the front face of a wave and the corner caught me on the lip. Stunned me and I went under. Swallowed a bunch of water and became disoriented. A couple of guys had to lead me back to the beach. I remembered my fear then, Mags, for the first time in years."

She nodded, remembering. When they were kids, he would barely get himself wet up to the knees.

"You were the one who got me out there in the first place, remember?"

She nodded. She'd pushed him to try even when he had that great fear. After a while, it seemed as if he had chosen the surf over her. Actually, he had.

He continued, "I hung it up after that accident, my fear of the water greater than my need to be out there making a name for myself. CeCe was furious."

"Is that what you meant the other day?"

He nodded. "To her, I was a big shot one day and just a guy who couldn't deliver the next."

"But surfing was your ... future."

"Not true. Not really. When I lost you, I lost everything— my reputation, my career ... you. I lost my most enthusiastic cheerleader the day you walked out of my life."

Maggie lowered her voice. "I was pushed out, Luke."

He nodded quickly. "Yes, I know. What I'm trying to say here, Mags, is I'm sorry. For everything I put you through and how my actions pushed you into a marriage as devoid of love as mine. I hope you can find a way to forgive me."

A sob escaped her. He was asking her to forgive him? After she had kept a secret from him all of these years? Every wall that she had built over the last ten years suddenly began to crumble.

He cupped her cheeks with his hands and brushed his lips across hers. "I love you, Mags."

Tears streamed down her cheeks as she kissed him back, softly at first, then hungrily, the chasm of years between them closing.

"A-hem."

Maggie jumped backward at the sound of Eva's interruption, but Luke stood steady, his arms still around her waist.

Eva's hands were on her hips, an incredulous expression on her face and what Maggie believed to be a bit of a twinkle in her eye. "What are you two doing?"

Eva. Her sweet, beautiful daughter, the child she'd loved from the very moment of her existence. Despite the messiness of life, Eva had been Maggie's evidence of light in the darkest of nights, her proof that God truly brought beauty from ashes.

Luke squeezed Maggie's hand, drawing her attention back to him. His gaze bored into hers. He was asking her a question with that one pleading look and it melted her like ice cream on a summer sidewalk. Slowly, she smiled and gave Luke a nod of encouragement.

With his gaze affixed to hers, he brought Maggie's hand to his mouth and kissed her fingers. Then Luke looked to where Eva stood, and reached an arm out to her. "Come over here, squirt. Your mother and I have something to tell you."

MAGGIE DUG her toes deep into the sand, one of her mother's old beach towels wrapped around her, and scanned the beach: surfers for miles. Or so it seemed. The wind was low and waves were high—a perfect day for a surf competition. In many ways, she was sixteen again, heady sleeplessness calling her from a warm bed early in the morning and out to the cool beach. The sun poked through the marine layer and somewhere up in that sky she could hear the buzz of media planes.

It was going to be a great day.

"I'm so excited!" Eva bounced on her heels, her teeth chattering from either the early morning air or a bit of trepidation. She wasn't sure which.

"This is going to be epic!" Siena said. She put her arm around her sister, causing a catch to form in Maggie's throat. "You and me are gonna kill it today. I can't wait!"

Maggie chuckled. "Sounds like you two are ready to go. Did you eat enough? Don't forget to put the leash on before you run into that surf. Oh, and make sure you keep an eye on the shoreline at all times."

"Mo-om!" Eva stared her down. She shook her head and quietly said, "So embarrassing."

Siena crouched down and looked directly into Maggie's eyes. "We're going to be okay, Mags. I promise. You're a nice momma."

Eva gagged a little, overacting, but she smiled too. She and Siena ran off toward the water then, their hands intertwined, each carrying a board under one arm.

Full-on tears mingled with an uncontrollable smile. Maggie hugged herself a little tighter.

"You look like a cat who's caught a salmon." Lacy plopped down on the sand, a mug of something hot and caffeinated in her hands. She drew a sip dramatically, like a dehydrated woman.

"I can't believe you brought your own espresso maker," Maggie said.

"Somebody had to bring some culture to this old place."

"There's a new bakery in town, th—"

"Gah. I know but no thanks. I very much doubt they can make espresso the right way."

Maggie turned her chin toward her sister. "You're a snob."

Lacy shrugged, a tiny smile on her face. "Your point?"

Maggie returned her gaze to the sea of surfers readying themselves for some friendly competition. "At least you're out here with the rest of the unwashed."

"Ha. Speak for yourself. I've already had a shower today."

"I thought I smelled something floral." Maggie wrinkled her nose. "It's competing with the espresso aroma, you know."

Lacy laughed. "Look at you. So discriminating!" She took another long sip of her latte before saying, "Contrary to what you might think, I'm very happy you've finally found your surfer prince, Maggie. Quite the shocking outcome, though."

"I'm sorry."

"Quit saying that. The over-apologizing is depressing."

Maggie swung a gaze at her sister. Was she serious?

Lacy flicked a side look. "All I can say is, I did not see it coming."

"That was by design, you know. Greg made me promise. We even brawled about it as our relationship began to deteriorate."

"Please. I never thought Greg was the father, anyway, especially after the way you ran into Rafael's arms after Luke was such a jerk."

Maggie gasped.

"What can I say? I've always thought Eva was Rafael's."

Maggie followed Lacy's gesture toward the shirtless wonder who was out on the beach this morning like just about everyone else. Though how he could stand there half-naked before the sun was overhead, she had no idea. Even surfers wore wetsuits ...

"Wait," Maggie said. "Is this why you've been so beastly to me lately?"

Lacy scrunched her eyes and gave Maggie a "c'mon" expression.

Maggie laughed, pointing at her sister. "You have a little crush on the bad boy, don't ya, Lace?"

"Ha. Always the big sister who thinks she knows everything." She held the mug to her lips and peered out over it in Rafael's direction. "I wouldn't call it a crush, but what can I say? I've always had an appreciation for his physique."

"Well, maybe now you'll have the opportunity to appreciate it more closely."

Lacy gave Maggie a tiny, wordless smile.

A pink paper bag dropped into the sand between them. Maggie jerked a look up.

Luke smiled. "Thought you could use some breakfast."

Lacy scoffed. "Oh, that's cute—you're own personal delivery service."

Maggie ignored her sister and grabbed the bag. She drew in an exaggerated breath. "Blueberry and sugar muffin tops. My favorite." She hopped to her feet and leaned into Luke. He smelled like musk, sea air, and neoprene. "You're my favorite."

He grinned. "Yeah?"

"Mm-hm." She kissed his lips.

"Gah! Please. Some of us have not had our breakfast yet and dry heaving is so unbecoming."

Luke snugged Maggie in for one more close hug before letting her go. "Gotta go. I'm supposed to be at the start."

Maggie touched his chin lightly. "You going to be okay?"

He flashed that wide smile at her again, the one that made her want to fold into him and never be set free. "You bet."

She watched him take off toward the shoreline, the tail of his zipper flapping behind him. Wave runners were at the ready, as were lifeguards who would watch from the sand, and teams with water and snacks.

"I have to give it to you, Mags. You really have fulfilled your calling."

"How so?"

"You fixed that boy right up. Isn't that what firstborn girls are supposed to do?"

Maggie's heart sank a little, a memory calling to her. "Maybe. Oh, but Lacy, I have such regret, especially where Mom was concerned."

Lacy was quiet a moment. "Well, kid, I do too."

"You do?"

Lacy wore a sobering look. "Yes."

Maggie nodded, not wishing to probe any deeper with

her often-stoic middle sister. She licked her lips, still looking out to sea, but her mind went suddenly elsewhere. "I think Mom wanted me to tell Luke and I didn't understand. Maybe she had some remorse about the way things were ... handled."

"What makes you say that?"

Maggie exhaled. "Aw, Lace. Recently I found some glittery artwork that she'd hidden away. It's the only piece of Eva's artwork that she saved—a picture Eva had drawn of herself and her father. Well, of the man she thought was him."

"Do you ever get the feeling like Mom and Dad wanted us to stay in the house for a reason? I admit, I'm a little creeped out by it all. But then again, I am also wondering what it is she has for me in there."

Maggie nodded. "Excellent way to put it. Grace told me about the books and then Jake seemed to come to terms with his rocky relationship with Dad after what he found." She shrugged. "Maybe you're right. Whenever she called me, she would say something like, 'Tell him. He needs to know.' I sensed she wasn't doing well for a long time, so I kept thinking she wanted me to tell Daddy something was wrong with her."

"And now?"

"And now ... I'm thinking Mom wanted me to come back to Colibri to confront my past."

"And now you have."

"And now I have."

They sat in the quiet a moment, the salt air warm and calming, when finally, Lacy said, "Mags? Do you think Dad knew Luke was Eva's father?"

"It's hard to say. He was always so … stoic."

Lacy scoffed. "Don't say it."

Maggie looked purposely at her sister now. "Don't say that you favor Dad in that area, you mean?"

Lacy groaned.

Maggie bumped Lacy with her shoulder. "Hey, well, I'm ecstatic at how things turned out after my month at the beach house. Let's hope you find what's hiding in plain sight for you too."

"Looks like they're about to start." Lacy stood and brushed off the sand from her legs.

"You're not sticking around to watch?"

"What … are you nuts? Of course, I am. I wouldn't miss seeing my niece show off on a surfboard for anything."

Maggie's heart lifted and crashed at about the same time, if that were possible. She was thrilled Lacy would stick around, but truthfully, when Luke told her that his campers were going to do a little exhibition at the start of the event, she could barely breathe, the memory of Eva and Siena's recent adventure too fresh.

"They'll be fine, Babe," Luke had assured her. "The staff has prepped them for this. Plus, I'll be nearby."

So she had agreed.

The beach was standing room only now, the anticipation of shoreside entertainment in the air. The team categories of beginner, intermediate, and advanced had congregated. And there was a special intergenerational category for the showoffs in the bunch. Each team would have fifteen minutes to catch waves and show what they could do.

But first, the tweens who had attended Luke's surf camp would do their exhibition run.

Lacy tsked. "Chill out, sis. Your daughters have surfing in their veins."

Maggie jerked a look at Lacy.

"I know nothing's official yet, but from what I've seen the past couple of days, you, Big Sis, are the mother that child never had."

Maggie pressed her lips together, suppressing the emotion rising in her throat.

A whistle blew and the kids ran into the surf, kicking up seawater and causing spectators to cheer. Maggie searched for the girls, thankful that she'd insisted on buying them new wetsuits, each with a different brightly colored stripe.

"Humor me," she'd said to Luke when he'd held up Siena's "perfectly acceptable" all-black wetsuit.

For the next ten minutes, the kids spread out and did what surfers do more than anything: they waited for the perfect wave. Both Eva and Siena caught different ones, each standing up for at least two seconds.

Lacy cupped her mouth and bellowed out the loudest "woo-hoo-hoo" that Maggie had ever heard.

Maggie shrank back, laughing. "Who *are* you and what have you done with my *very* proper sister?"

"Being proper has nothing to do with shutting one's mouth—and everything to do with knowing when to make one's voice heard."

"Um, okay."

Lacy laughed and bumped Maggie with her hip.

A second piercing whistle broke through the crowd indicating this heat was done and another would soon begin. Secretly, Maggie was happy the girls were done and would be coming in now. She'd packed snacks so they could sit on the beach with her and watch the competition. Maggie pulled towels from the bag over her arm and readied them for the girls.

"I wonder what they're doing," Lacy said.

Maggie quirked a look at her. "What who's doing?"

Lacy flicked her chin toward the ocean. "All the kids are lining up out there. I think they're pointing at ... you."

"What?" The morning sun had emerged, adding dapples of sunlight on the water. Maggie squinted, shading her eyes with a hand, and searched for Eva and Siena among the group bobbing out there. It did almost look like they were pointing this way. Maggie glanced at Lacy who had a silly smile on her face, her tongue stuck out between her teeth.

"Sure looks like they are trying to get your attention, Mags."

The buzz of one of those media planes flying lower than normal caught her attention, as did the collective shout from the kids in the water. She looked up at the plane and back at the kids who were all shouting and pointing up at that overhead plane.

"Look closer," Luke whispered.

Maggie jerked her chin to find Luke standing next to her. Her sister had vanished.

He chuckled. "Not at me. Up there."

She followed his gaze to the plane, this time noticing a flowing banner flying behind it. She kept watching until the plane's banner came fully into view. It read: *Will You Marry Me, Mags?*

Maggie gasped. She turned her gaze on him. "I wonder who it's from?"

Luke growled and scooped her into his neoprene-clad

arms. "It's not from Rafael—I can tell you that," he said, his voice deep and full of laughter.

Maggie feigned surprise. "It's not?"

He cinched her closer again, their mouths inches apart. Maggie reached up and touched the scar above his lip. She reveled in the brush of his warm breath on her face, the glint of pure joy—mixed with a little mischief—in his eyes. "It's you, Mags," he said. "It's always been you. Say you'll marry me."

She licked her lips, her smile giving her away. "I'll marry you," she whispered. "It's always been yes."

With a whoop, Luke lifted Maggie from the sand, his strong hands holding her up in the air like she was Jennifer Grey and he her Patrick Swayze. Siena and Eva showed up giggling and carrying on, telling Luke to put her down. Pretty soon a swarm of well-wishers had gathered around them, including Lacy, who hissed, "Okay, we get it, nobody puts Baby in the corner."

Luke laughed heartily and put Maggie back on the ground, though truthfully, as she accepted the hugs and congratulations from those who had gathered around them, her feet could still not feel the earth beneath them.

A whistle blew, announcing the start of the next phase of the contest. As the crowd around them thinned, Maggie found herself blinking back tears that had been gathering all morning. Only these weren't from heartache. She glanced up at Luke, whose eyes had not left her face, and all she felt was gratitude ... for a second chance at love.

ALSO BY JULIE CAROBINI

Julie's books are available wherever books are sold, including her
online shop: JulieCarobini.com

Beach House Romances

Beach Sunrise (book 1)

Beach Memories (book 2)

Beach Secrets (book 3)

Beach Sunset (book 4)

Beach Music (book 5)

Standalone

Reunion in Saltwater Beach

Hollywood by the Sea Novels

Chasing Valentino (book 1)

Finding Stardust (book 2)

Sea Glass Inn Novels

Walking on Sea Glass (book 1)

Runaway Tide (book 2)

Windswept (book 3)

Beneath a Billion Stars (book 4)

A Sea Glass Christmas (book 5)

Otter Bay Novels

Sweet Waters (book 1)

A Shore Thing (book 2)

Fade to Blue (book 3)

The Otter Bay Novel Collection (books 1-3)

The Chocolate Series

Chocolate Beach (book 1)

Truffles by the Sea (book 2)

Mocha Sunrise (book 3)

Cottage Grove Cozy Mysteries

The Christmas Thief (book 1)

The Christmas Killer (book 2)

The Christmas Heist (book 3)

Cottage Grove Mysteries (books 1-3)

ABOUT THE AUTHOR

JULIE CAROBINI is the author of 22+ inspirational beach romances. Her books feature captivating heroines, endearing heroes, and a cast of quirky friends, all bound together by the secrets they keep. Her bestselling titles include *Walking on Sea Glass, Runaway Tide,* and *Reunion in Saltwater Beach.* Julie has received awards for writing and editing from The National League of American Pen Women and ACFW, and she is a double finalist for the ACFW Carol Award. She is the mother of three grown kids and lives on the California coast with her husband, Dan, and their rescue pup, Dancer.

Please visit her at
www.juliecarobini.com

Made in the USA
Columbia, SC
11 June 2024

36452799R20109